AF133286

Praise for Emma Read

Gloriously spooky and utterly splendid.
HANA TOOKE

The peril is real, the setting is out of this world, and the mystery unfolds and teases like diabolical clockwork.
MICHAEL MANN

A fun, fresh and delightfully creepy mystery that sucked me in like a sinkhole and never let go.
AMY McCAW

A deliciously creepy, shocking thrill-ride of a book.
SOPHIE WILLS

It's an absolute corker.
THE PHOENIX

Brings great humour and insight . . . a charming and thoughtful read.
THE SCOTSMAN

As fearless and charismatic a crew of characters as any others you might come across in children's fiction.
THE IRISH TIMES

A MESSAGE FROM CHICKEN HOUSE

When I was a boy, I was obsessed with John Wyndham's *The Day of the Triffids* – and the horrifying plants that invaded the Earth! Now, I am not saying that Emma's houseplants are at all suspicious, but what starts with a normal family Christmas ends up as a full-scale creepy thriller . . . can our unfortunate heroes save the day? Grab the mince pies, dive in and find out!

BARRY CUNNINGHAM
Publisher
Chicken House

SILENT NIGHT

EMMA READ

Chicken House

2 Palmer Street, Frome, Somerset BA11 1DS

First published in the UK in 2025
Chicken House
2 Palmer Street
Frome, Somerset BA11 1DS
United Kingdom
www.chickenhousebooks.com

Chicken House/Scholastic Ireland, 89E Lagan Road, Dublin Industrial Estate,
Glasnevin, Dublin D11 HP5F, Republic of Ireland

Text © Emma Read 2025
Illustration © Tom Clohosy Cole Ltd 2025

The moral rights of the author and illustrator have been asserted.

All rights reserved.
No part of this publication may be reproduced, transmitted, downloaded, decompiled, reverse engineered, used to train any artificial intelligence technologies, or stored in or introduced into any information storage and retrieval system, in any form or by any means, whether electronic or mechanical, now known or hereafter invented, without the express written permission of the publisher. Subject to EU law the publisher expressly reserves this work from the text and data mining exception.

This book is a work of fiction. Names, characters, businesses, organizations, places, events and incidents are either the product of the author's imagination or used in a fictitious manner. Any resemblance to actual persons, living or dead, events or locales is purely coincidental.

For safety or quality concerns:
UK: www.chickenhousebooks.com/productinformation
EU: www.scholastic.ie/productinformation

Cover design by Steve Wells
Interior design by Steve Wells
Typeset by Dorchester Typesetting Group Ltd
Printed in the UK by Clays, Elcograf S.p.A

FSC
www.fsc.org
MIX
Paper | Supporting responsible forestry
FSC® C018072

1 3 5 7 9 10 8 6 4 2

A CIP catalogue record for this book is available from the British Library.

PB ISBN 978-1-913322-79-3
eISBN 978-1-917171-26-7

To Dad, for the Triffids

1

OH, CHRISTMAS TREE

24 December

At 4 p.m., the Christmas lights came on automatically, and I practically jumped out of my skin. It was especially unfortunate as I was underneath the tree, lying on my front, intently focused on the presents. I wasn't touching them (of course), but trying to figure out if the red-wrapped box at the back was big enough to be a PlayStation. The whole tree jingled, and I felt my hair fill with fir needles. A sparkly glass mushroom dropped to the carpet beside me.

It wasn't just the lights coming on that'd made me jump, though – I was on edge, away from home and out of my comfort zone.

'You trying to use X-ray vision on those gifts again, Mase?' said Dad, hovering in the doorway of the family room. 'Don't bother, they're all socks.'

'Even that one?' I pointed to a long gift-wrapped tube – clearly a poster.

I was grateful he'd not made a big thing of my obvious anxiety.

'It's a tube of socks.' Dad grinned.

'And that one?' I waved my glasses at a thin, flat present wrapped in reused stripy paper.

'Of course! Very thin, flat socks.'

Mum came in from the kitchen and topped up Dad's glass of Prosecco, as wind and rain hammered against the old cottage windows. 'This weather!' she said. 'Thank goodness we got here when we did.' She peered out of the window, not that she could've seen far through the lashing Storm Elena was giving South Wales. 'I'm a bit worried about the others driving in this. Send them another text will you, Ed?' She drew the curtains and gave me a reassuring wink. 'You OK, Mase? If it all gets a bit much, just nip upstairs for a bit. Christmas is stressful for everyone, but we'll take it like we do everything, right? One step at a time.' A car horn sounded from outside the house that wasn't home. 'Oh! They're here!' Mum sighed in relief.

Dad took a hearty swig of fizz, put his glass on a side table – beside one of the many weird miniature Christmas trees that decorated the house – and clapped his hands together. 'Only three hours late; that's pretty good for your Aunty Suzie, storm or no storm. Now the celebrations can properly start.'

I shuffled closer to the tree, keeping my back to the gifts, almost protective. Outside, car doors slammed and then people (and two burly chocolate Labradors) bundled loudly into the hallway. Bags thumped on to the carpet, raincoats were handed off and greetings of 'Happy Christmas Eve!' were muffled by hugs. Dad squeezed my shoulder.

Mum's sister, Suzie, found me first. 'Come on, Masen – give yer bestie aunty a hug. *It's Christmas!*'

I got to my feet and succumbed to an embrace of perfume, fruitcake and damp air.

'You're taller than ever!' She turned to Mum. 'Isn't he so tall now, Taylor? And ooh, what's that . . .?' I knew what was coming as she grabbed my chin. 'Getting a little fluffy, aren't we? And not even fourteen yet.'

I cringed – my cousin Conor was right behind her, wearing his trademark tube socks and jorts. He was stroking his chin in an exaggerated way and sniggering. Aunty Suzie didn't notice. 'They grow up that quick these days.' She laughed loudly, but even though I was the butt of the joke, I smiled. Suzie's loud personality was everything that would normally make me shrink into myself, but my aunt got a pass. Her laughter was infectious. 'And where's my little Jossy?' she asked, accepting a glass of Prosecco, still in the hallway. My younger brother, dressed in a suit and tie, launched himself down the stairs and into a hug.

With Jos still attached to her, Suzie wafted around the family room of the holiday cottage. 'This place is gorgeous! Did they decorate it for you? You don't always get that in an Airbnb.' She surveyed the room, touching the fake ivy and ruffling the shiny garlands. Then, she spotted the strange miniature tree on the coffee table. 'That's . . . um, cute too.' She shrugged. 'If you like that sort of thing.'

The 'cute' little Christmas trees were in every room. They were about thirty centimetres tall –

sort of A4 size if you included the red sparkly pot – and covered with . . . well, no one could agree quite what. I said flowers, Dad said fungi and Mum went for something in between. Each tree was heavy with rubbery blooms made of fat, juicy petals in various colours. And they had weird markings that shimmered and rippled through a colour spectrum – a bit like deep-sea creatures. They even glowed in the dark. I wouldn't call them cute, especially as they smelt so bad. A cross between air freshener and mouldy bread.

'Strange, isn't it?' Mum ran her fingers over velvety, vivid pink petals. 'Like something one of the kids would've made at a Christmas craft fayre. But out of Play-Doh.'

'Maybe you shouldn't touch it,' said Suzie, wrinkling her face.

Mum wiped her fingers on her jeans. 'There's loads of them. I reckon the owner ordered too many by mistake and dumped them all here. They're in the bathrooms, the hall . . .' The dogs, Fran and Kika, wandered into the family room, sniffing everything but avoiding the little trees, looking at them suspiciously.

'Good girls, no eating the weird plants,' Suzie said to the dogs. 'That would be too much drama for Christmas Eve. I would like to chill this holiday.'

Me too, Suzie.

But as I watched the rest of the newly arrived gang flood into the sitting room, chilling seemed utterly impossible. Conor patted me on the head, then started wrestling on the sofa with his dad, my uncle Mikael. My dad's two brothers, Scott and Benedict, and Benedict's husband Bradlee sat on the other sofa and broke into a loud rendition of 'Last Christmas'. The dogs chased Jos around the coffee table, licking any available bare skin and knocking everything flying. Mikael's elderly mother Nanny Sasha was the only one who was quiet. She ambled in and plonked herself on the nearest chair, earbuds in, probably listening to the *Wicked* soundtrack, if I knew her.

We were a happy family, but a loud one. And a big one – hence the cottage: the only place Mum could find that was big enough to seat us around one table. I'd only agreed to it because Mum promised I'd have somewhere to retreat. I adored my family (well, except Conor) but sometimes I just needed a break from them. So, Jos, Conor and I were going to sleep on our own in the caravan parked on the drive. I had a bolthole and we all got to feel a bit more independent. I'd already checked it out too, and there were absolutely no weird little mushroom-trees.

2

ONE MORE SLEEP

24 December

'Mase, love – come and help me bring the food out, will you?' Mum ushered me to the calm of the kitchen, where she put nibbles on plates while I took some me-time. I counted to ten, breathing slowly to recentre and then, when I felt better, between us we transported enough food to feed a small army. Finally! This was the highlight of Christmas Eve: cold meats, pigs in blankets, cheese, crackers, little jars of chutneys and of course . . . a huge tub of Celebrations.

Fran the Labrador was straight in before we could stop her, whipping a slice of beef off the plate and wolfing it down like it was from the last cow on Earth.

Suzie squealed and Benedict practically threw himself at the dog, comedy-fashion, bumping into the coffee table and knocking the mushroom-tree on to the floor.

'Mind the Prosecco!' cried Mum, revealing her priorities. 'And someone hand me that plant before Fran grabs it. I'll put it with the others in the kitchen.'

Scott hauled Fran out from underneath Benedict, who then handed Mum the now-dishevelled mushroom-tree. Kika barked enthusiastically from Bradlee's lap as Conor threw a slice of ham to her. *Mayhem.* Nanny Sasha was not impressed.

'Conor Haarket! You behave yourself now, you hear. We'll have none of that throwing food about. Your aunty has gone to a lot of care and expense.' Nanny Sasha was small, but scary when she wanted to be, and Conor blushed redder than Bradlee's Santa hat at being scolded.

I smirked. 'Can I get you a drink, Nanny Sasha?' She was now officially my favourite family member.

After that, Christmas Eve continued much as it usually did, starting with us all watching an ancient

James Bond movie while eating our body weight in chocolate. The storm continued to grow and although Mikael said it was out to sea, it sounded like it was getting closer.

Nanny Sasha nodded off in her chair. We played a board game, argued about not wearing matching pyjamas any more (thirteen years old was where I drew the line, no matter what Suzie said) and then Conor made us listen to his latest playlist until we were saved by the power going out, plunging us into silence and sudden darkness.

'That storm!' said Mikael. Lightning flashed through the crack in the curtains, and we counted to ten before we heard the rumble. The next time it happened, we only counted to nine.

'Ooh, it's just like when we were kids,' said Suzie gleefully. 'Christmas by candlelight. It'll be lovely.'

'It won't be if we can't cook dinner tomorrow,' said Benedict.

'Or get the radiators on,' agreed Scott, reaching for his cardigan on the back of the sofa.

'Isn't there gas central heating?' asked Bradlee.

'Nope. All electric out here – the gas doesn't come this far down,' said Mum, looking worried.

'Anyone got any matches?'

'Remind me, why did we have to come to the countryside?' moaned Conor.

Mum sighed. 'I chose the place because it was isolated – good for a proper getaway from it all, from the city . . . maybe that was a bad idea.'

Lightning flashed outside again. Jos counted to four and we jumped as the boom of the thunder roared closer.

'At least the kids will be fine,' said Mum. 'There's a battery-powered heater in the caravan. Kids, why don't you get off to bed? Might as well. And tomorrow morning it'll be Christmas!' She touched Jossy's cheek lovingly.

'It's nearly Christmas now,' I said, holding my phone and showing off the time. 'Can we stay up until midnight?' Conor, Jos and I gave our parents a pleading look.

'I don't think so,' said Mum, hunting through the dresser drawers for matches. 'But you can open a present now. Since that's what you're really asking. Just one!'

Using the torch on my phone, I dived for the big present at the back, but Dad was too quick.

'Something small.' He handed me a little square box which I could tell was from Mum by the recycled brown paper it was wrapped in. She'd decorated it with a drawing of a map, which was a clue to the present inside.

Suzie had found a lighter and lit some cinnamon-scented candles, and in the flickering light, I carefully opened my present, as Conor and Jos tore into theirs. Conor's gift was a pair of stripy, knee-high wellie socks, and I pointedly did not look at Dad, who I could tell was stifling a laugh. Conor scowled at me, then turned to Suzie.

'Is this what I think it is?' He was feeling the socks, eager hopefulness on his face. I often found my cousin's interactions confusing, but this was next level. Stranger still, he then pulled a bunch of tent pegs out of the socks, which I assumed were a family joke, as he and his parents were all excessively happy about it.

'I can go?' asked Conor.

Suzie's leg jiggled and she almost spilt her drink. 'You can go! The rest of the tent isn't wrapped – it was too big.'

Go where?

Conor pulled on the ridiculous stripy socks and flew at his mum, properly spilling her Prosecco now. 'Thanks, Mum! I'll be fine, I promise. Yes! I'm going to Glasto!'

Ah, of course. Conor had been begging to go to a festival with his friends, but as he'd still only be seventeen next summer, he needed his parents' consent. With that little mystery solved, I looked across at Jos, who was even more excited than Conor, if that was possible. It was the first year he'd been allowed to stay up as late as (almost) midnight, now he was nine, and the thrill was practically bursting out of him. He could barely speak as he showed each of us the penknife Uncle Mikael had bought him. He opened up all the parts and started waving the serrated blade at Nanny Sasha. Uncle Benedict made a grab for it, suggesting he saved it for 'outside time', and Aunty Suzie went off on one of her laughing fits again. With the penknife put in a safe place, she pulled Jos into a hug. 'Jossy, never change,' she said.

Then it was my turn. I smoothed out Mum's wrapping-paper map, put it aside to save for later and opened the box, holding out my gift for everyone to see.

'Well, with that, my tent and Jos's knife, we're all set for the zombie apocalypse,' said Conor, with a thumbs up.

3

THE BIG DAY

24–25 December

'Mase, help Conor take his stuff over to the caravan, please,' said Mum, yawning.

Conor grabbed his holdall. 'No problem, Aunty Tay, I'm a big strong lad!' he said, looking down at me like he thought I was a skinny, weak 'lad'.

'Come on, Jos,' said Mum as my little brother made a valiant attempt at procrastination by hugging all the uncles, Aunty Suzie, Nanny Sasha and the two dogs.

'Sleep tight and Santa will come. Tomorrow will be full of surprises,' said Suzie. She'd found one of the mushroom-trees in her bedroom and was now holding it at arm's length as if looking for somewhere to put it, far away from her.

Preferably the bin.

Mum opened the door and the roar of Storm Elena hit us. She threw our raincoats over our heads. 'Get the heater on in the caravan as soon as you get in – it'll be chilly in there. I'm glad I brought the winter duvets now.' She popped an umbrella open over Jos and handed it to me, but as soon as the door clicked softly closed behind us it turned inside out in the wind.

Giggling against the furious sideways rain, we bundled into the caravan and I got the wall heater on and closed all the curtains. 'Don't worry about your teeth, Jos, you can double brush in the morning,' I said, tucking him into the bottom bunk and climbing to the top, sliding Mum's present under the pillow. I half wished I'd brought Bear with me, but there was no way I was risking ridicule from Conor when he saw I still slept with a cuddly toy. I placed my hand on top of the gift instead – an antique compass, the brass slightly worn, the face crystal clear. It steadied my anxious heart until I realized I hadn't even thanked Mum for it.

*

I woke sweating, and kicked off the duvet, silently scolding myself for putting the infrared heater on full blast; not very eco-friendly of me and kinda dangerous.

But I didn't worry for too long because IT WAS CHRISTMAS!

I listened to the stillness of the morning. The storm had obviously stopped and Jos and Conor were still asleep so I stealth-dropped to the floor, left the curtains closed and went into the little kitchen. The caravan was pretty neat – like a mini home, with all the essentials, and I imagined what it would be like to live independently, with no adults controlling my life. It made me feel quite mature and surprisingly un-anxious.

I grabbed a mug from the cupboard above the little sink, poured a glass of water, and checked the time. Nine thirty on Christmas morning. Excitement fizzed inside me at the thought of the day, the presents, the food. And not a hint of worry. I pictured the adults, probably still in their PJs and wanting 'coffee first' . . . assuming the power was back. Visualizing the expected noise and chaos helped me stay focused.

I'll get the kettle on and thank Mum for my compass.

As quietly as I could, I slipped on my dressing gown, popped open the latch on the caravan door and stepped down with a crunch.

SNOW!

It was as though the morning couldn't be any more perfect. My heart skipped at the thought of that maybe-PlayStation under the tree, tear-and-share pastries, Biscoff stars – maybe I'd even be allowed a caramel latte. Pulling the caravan door closed, I began to register how cold the air was inside my nostrils. I quickly checked my phone to see the temperature but there was no Wi-Fi.

The trees were all glittering, and so was the caravan.

Then as I stared, more flakes of snow began to fall, scudding about in the low breeze.

It's snowing on Christmas Day!

I ran to the front door of the cottage, which was cracked open, despite the chill. As I crunched across the gravel, excitement built rapidly and I didn't see the pot until I tripped over it. It was a mini mushroom-tree. But it was very dead. I crouched down to pick it up.

The tree was shrivelled. It hadn't been big to start with but now it was no larger than my fist – a hard, knobbly stump, black and streaked with grey. The flower-mushrooms were all gone and there were gooey patches of something black and sticky . . . perhaps all that was left of the blooms. I thought of Aunty Suzie holding it the night before like it was one of Fran or Kika's poo bags. She must've put it outside, fed up with the smell.

I hope she doesn't get into trouble.

A fat snowflake landed in the sticky mess.

'Mum! Dad! It's snowing – on Christmas!'

One absolute truth about snow is that it trumps everything else – you're sleeping, get up; watching a movie, hit pause; you need coffee because you were up super late on Christmas Eve playing poker for jellybeans (looking at you, my family), who cares – it's SNOW!

I raced into the house. 'Mum?'

There was no answer.

They must be outside too, watching the snow fall.

I dashed through the kitchen and into the back

garden. The grass crackled and snapped beneath my feet and I was very aware I was wearing my slippers. 'Mum? Dad?'

Still no answer.

'Aunt Suzie? Uncle Bradlee?'

Nothing.

The words hung in the air like speech bubbles. It was so quiet. And so cold.

Properly shivering, I went back inside the cottage and closed the bifold doors, which were slung wide open, almost like they'd been pushed aside in a hurry.

They can't all still be in bed?

They weren't. I checked the bedrooms and the family room. All empty. The whole house was freezing, as if the doors had been open for hours. I grabbed one of Dad's hoodies and pulled it on, tugging the hood up for extra warmth.

Then I checked the cars – maybe they'd gone for a drive?

A horrible thought struck me: what if something had happened to Nanny Sasha in the night? Had they gone to A and E? She was pretty old. A lump lodged in my throat. Maybe she shouldn't have eaten all those mini Snickers.

But they wouldn't all *go, not without telling the three of us in the caravan, would they?*

And they hadn't. The cars were on the drive.

I dashed back to the caravan to find Jos brushing his teeth – a double brush – and Conor pulling on an old manga hoody. 'Jeez, Mase – shut the door, mate. It's bloody freezing!'

'Everyone's gone,' I said, breathless.

'What?' He pushed the hood back.

'I mean there's no one in the cottage. The front door was open . . . and the patio doors.'

Conor pulled the tiny curtains back and looked out of the window. 'And? They've probably taken the dogs for a walk.'

I hadn't thought of that.

As I got dressed, Conor carried on, seeming to enjoy making me feel silly for worrying. 'Seriously, chill out, mate. Do you think they've run off on Christmas morning? I bet Dad's made them all go out for some fresh air. He loves to get you London types out for an invigorating hike.'

I relaxed a bit. *Yes. That had to be it.* It was exactly the sort of Scandinavian thing Mikael would do.

‘Anyway, I’m starving. Let’s get breakfast.’ Conor was out of the door before I could protest. I wanted breakfast as much as he did, but the whole family did it *together*. My money was on Conor wanting to swig a glass of leftover Prosecco before anyone saw him.

‘Pop your coat on, Jos, it’s been snowing and it’s cold inside ’cause the doors were left open,’ I said, and we followed Conor.

4

IT'S CHRISTMAS!

25 December

Jos stood in the doorway to the kitchen, his mouth hanging open.

Suzie wasn't going to be the only one in trouble. *All* the little Christmas trees were dead. Just like the one on the doorstep, they were withered in their pots, gnarled like decaying, bony hands reaching up out of a jolly snowflake-covered pot. It was more Halloween than Christmas. The ones still left in the family room were the same.

Mum would be gutted. And would it mean we wouldn't get our deposit back?

Conor twisted his face and turned his hands into claws. 'Welcome to Dead House at Christmas!' He cackled. 'Not quite the vibe your mum was going for.' He laughed and I hated him for it. Why did they have to bring him?

'Maybe this is why they left?' suggested Jos. 'Maybe they went to the shops to get more.'

'No, Jos. It's Christmas Day,' I said. 'There aren't any shops open. And even if there were, I've never seen plants like this in a shop.' I took a closer look at one, removing it from its once-cosy spot on the bookcase. Like the rest, it was withered and crusty, and dripping with gloop. It made sense that the one outside had died but . . . wait . . . was it dead?

I peered closer. The black goo was moving, pulsing slightly and glistening in the pale morning light. Suddenly one of the blobs flexed and turned itself inside out, coughing up more oozing goo from inside itself. It was so disgusting I screamed and dropped the pot. It bounced on the carpet, spilling soil, black ooze and the remains of the shrivelled stump on to the floor.

Conor, of course, roared with laughter.

I looked back at the blobs and they were still.

'Shut up.' It was all I could manage. I couldn't think of anything clever to say, because I was too busy wondering if I'd imagined it. I was so jumpy; what if my mind was playing tricks? I could feel myself getting angry at Conor and I tried to calm down but the smell of the mushroom-trees was even worse now they were dead, and my head spun at the thought of Mum's perfect family Christmas being spoilt. I touched the compass in my dressing-gown pocket, and my insides untwisted a little. Maybe Jos was right, and the plant carnage did have something to do with why they were gone.

Jos tried to put the telly on but the power was still out. Instead, he curled up on a sofa with his phone to edit some videos for his YouTube channel. Conor and I shrugged and went on our phones too. Dad would call us phone-zombies for scrolling on Christmas Day and I felt a bit guilty, but there wasn't anything else to do except stare at the presents under the tree. After about ten minutes I looked up to see Conor doing just that. He slid off the sofa, crawled to the tree and reached to the back, pulling out a gift. He looked at us, shrugged, then unwrapped it. I could see Jos was desperate to do the same, but I didn't budge. I wanted that PlayStation so badly, but rules were rules. *After* breakfast. *With* family.

Half an hour passed and my stomach was practically devouring itself and Jos was getting whiny. There was no point calling Mum and Dad; their phones were in the kitchen, plugged in but not charging. Conor tried to call his dad, and it was then we realized there was no phone signal.

'Do you think the storm took out the phone masts?' I said to no one in particular. 'OK, I'm going to make Jos some cereal,' I added when no one answered. 'Want anything?'

'Yeah. A ride out of here,' said Conor. 'Man, I wish there was a way to make coffee.' He'd opened two more presents and was proudly flashing his new FitWatch.

I sighed and left him and Jos sprawled out in the front room like they owned the place.

In the kitchen, I grabbed a box of Rice Krispies and then some rapidly warming milk from the fridge, thinking I ought to pop the milk outside to keep cold. Then I got cheese straws and a plateful of veggie sausage rolls for me and Conor. Breakfast of champions.

The kitchen felt so big and quiet and I hurried

back to the family room. Where could they be? The early morning 'invigorating' hike did seem like the best explanation – if I didn't think too long about Nanny Sasha – but it didn't stop my breathing being all up in my chest. I put two fingers to my pulse and my heart was racing.

No. There's a simple reason why they're gone. And why they've left us behind.

I tried to push aside the thought that it must've involved some kind of emergency, because Mum and Dad wouldn't leave Jos behind without an explanation.

But it was only ten forty. They'd be back any minute and Mum would be all hugs over Jossy, and Aunty Suzie would spill the beans in the most dramatic way and we'd all laugh about it and the dogs would be . . .

The dogs! Oh no! What if that stupid mushroom-tree has poisoned them and they've rushed to the vet?

'Do you think the dogs ate the little trees? And that's why they're dead?'

Jos gasped. 'Are Fran and Kika dead?'

Conor tutted. 'No, silly! Go back to your dumb-ass Tuber – the dogs aren't dead, the plants are.'

I bristled when Conor called Jos silly.

'They'll be back soon. Let's just make the most of it. Wanna listen to Høyt?' Conor stuffed his face with sausage rolls and cracked open the rest of the Celebrations.

'No thanks,' I said, less than keen for more Norwegian pop music.

'Mase,' Jos was getting even more whiny, 'can *I* open a present? Conor's opened four already! Just a little one.'

'No, Jos. You have to say thank you to the person who gave you the gift as you open it, so they can see you're happy and grateful.'

'But they're not here.'

No, they're not.

'Do you think they went missing, Mase?' Jos was fiddling with his fingers, which he always did if something was worrying him.

'Don't worry, Jos. Hey, why don't we watch one of the movies Dad downloaded on the iPad for the car journey? They're sure to turn up just as we're getting into it.'

We chose a new Netflix original about dragons that we just about all agreed on, and settled down to wait for the tidal wave of noise and barking that was sure to come.

Any moment.

5

QUIET TIME

25 December

The movie ended and Conor switched off the telly. No one said anything. The dragons had been defeated and the heroes had saved the day. But we were still alone.

What the hell is going on? Where are Mum and Dad? Why? Why would they leave us?

There were no answers to my questions, because no matter what terrible thing might have happened, one of them would have called, or returned home.

'It's way after twelve o'clock. Mum and Dad usually start making Christmas dinner around now, don't they? They wouldn't not make Christmas dinner?' Jos was really twiddling his fingers now.

'I'm going to go to the main road to see if I can see anything . . . anyone,' I said.

'I'll come too,' said Conor.

'No, you stay with Jos, please. I'll only be ten minutes or so.'

'No way, man. I'm not the babysitter.'

'And I'm not a baby,' insisted Jos. 'Can we all go?'

'No, someone needs to be here in case they . . . I mean, *when* they come back.'

Jos looked like he was going to cry or be sick.

'We'll leave a note.'

I zipped up Jos's puffer jacket and we crunched on to the gravel, to the end of the drive, then the narrow road at the bottom. The trees were still glittering with snow and the air stung my throat. Even in my pockets, my hands were beginning to tingle.

We walked for five minutes to the main road. It wasn't exactly main, main, but it led to the village one way, and further down towards the coast the other. It was the only way traffic ran . . . but there was none.

'It's Christmas Day – no one's driving anyway. This doesn't tell us anything,' said Conor. 'And I'm freezing. I'm going back, I'm going to open the rest of my presents and yours if you don't want them.'

'Don't you dare,' I said. 'Go back if you want. I'm going to walk a bit further and see if I can find any houses. Jossy – you go back with Conor. It's too cold out here.'

But Jos was stubborn and I didn't push very hard. To be honest, I preferred to have him with me – for company, but also . . . I didn't trust Conor to look after him properly.

We walked east, according to my compass, until we came to the edge of Knelston, the closest village to the cottage. I saw Jos physically relax as we came upon the first house – a small place, stuck out on its own, on the edge of the village – which had flashing Christmas lights in the front hedge. I held his hand as we walked up the path, intending to knock on the door, except . . . the front door was open.

Like ours had been.

It was too cold for the door to be left open on purpose.

I shook the thought away.

'Hello?' I called, knocking anyway. 'Is there anyone home? Err, Merry Christmas.'

The house was silent, the hallway dark and gloomy.

Coats hung by the door, there were pictures on the walls – the house looked normal, only . . . empty and cold. I flipped the light switch but the power was out here, too. The Christmas lights had given me hope but a quick glance confirmed they were solar-powered.

'I'm going in . . . there might be someone in trouble inside,' I said. That wasn't my absolute honest reason for wanting to enter the house, but it was a part of it and the more I thought about it the more that part grew. But Jos shook his head.

'We can't go in someone's house. We're not invited.'

I fidgeted on the doormat. 'Stay here. I'll just be a sec.'

Jos grabbed my coat. 'No! Don't leave me out here, Mase,' he whispered. 'I don't like this. It's too quiet.' I looked around at the grey trees, gripped by ice, at the wide, lonely fields, at the dead sky.

'Don't be silly.' I smiled confidently and bent to his level. 'I'll be right back.'

The hallway was short with a small kitchen-diner

to the right and the living room to the left. As I ventured in, I continued to call 'Hello' in case I surprised anyone, but the place seemed deserted. The curtains in the living room were closed, with just a sliver of light shining through, but it revealed nothing but dust motes hanging lazily in the air, along with the silence.

My breath led the way, vapour puffing out before me like a speeding old steam train.

I lingered at the bottom of the stairs. Going up to the bedrooms felt wrong, but I had to check.

'Hello? I'm coming up the stairs . . . I hope that's OK.'

One step at a time.

The first step creaked and I paused. Maybe Jos was right – I shouldn't be here in a stranger's house. If someone came home and was angry, I'd be trapped on the first floor. Would they believe I wasn't a burglar? Would they call the police, or just jump on me? I tried not to think about it as I pushed open the door to my right to reveal the bathroom. It was dark, but I could make out two toothbrushes, towels on the radiator, the blind down . . . I avoided looking at the mirror, suddenly afraid of what I might see behind me.

A small bedroom to the left was empty, the bed made, and the curtains drawn there too. The whole upstairs was dark and so still, and an unwanted image settled in my head of the two people who lived here in their beds . . . dead, withered and decayed like the mushroom-trees.

I swallowed and pushed open the third door, at the end of the hall.

'Hello,' I whispered. My voice caught in my throat.

As my eyes adjusted to the gloom I saw a double bed, the duvet bunched up over a lump in the middle. About the size of a person.

I coughed, half to announce my presence, half in fright.

What am I doing?

I hovered in the doorway, frozen by indecision. I didn't want to see a dead body, not on Christmas Day, not any day.

You have to do the right thing, Mase. If they are dead, you have to call the police.

I skirted the wall, staying as far away as possible from the shape on the bed, and tugged the curtains aside. Daylight poured in, revealing . . . an empty bed. The lump was just the duvet piled high from both sides as if two occupants had pushed it aside at the same time.

I opened the window and gulped in the frigid air to stop myself from being sick with the tension. Jos was below and I called out to him, giving him a thumbs up. Poor thing, he jumped a mile in the air but then waved back. In the distance, I could see the rest of the village, about a quarter of a kilometre further on. It looked deserted. But then, it was Christmas Day. I ducked back into the room. There was nothing here and no one who could help us. It was time to go.

I was about to leave when I spotted something else. On the bedside tables, either side of the bed, were blackened stumps of mushroom-trees.

6

ARRIVAL

25 December

Jos and I pushed on to the edge of the village and knocked on the wide-open doors of four more houses – again, we got no answer. I didn't go inside to investigate – my heart was still racing from being in the first house. There was a gap in the buildings as we crossed a stream then, on the other side, a small petrol station. A large black family car was parked at a weird angle by the pumps – actually, more sort of left there than parked. It was empty too, and so was the little shop. A fox poked around in the bins out the back, knocking snow to the ground in white powdery puffs. I held Jos back to watch it. We stood like statues so as not to scare it off, but it just looked at us, bored and unbothered, and strolled off in its own time.

I tried my best to absorb some of Jossy's worries and we talked about how we'd surely arrive back at the cottage to find the family returned, the oven on, and all of us feeling properly foolish. I think he bought into it – well, as much as he still believed in the tooth fairy, but I knew it was a lie.

We could have gone further but Jos was cold and we were both getting more and more freaked out by all the nothing we found, so we headed back.

There would be nothing waiting for us at the cottage except Con—

My insides were suddenly colder than my outsides.

Conor.

He'd be there . . . right?

I dragged Jos, half jogging, up the drive, past the caravan, to the front door. I was relieved to see that it was closed, then immediately terrified when no one answered the bell.

I banged on the door and flapped the letterbox but got no reply. Jos was shivering. We had to get back inside.

'Is Conor gone too?' Jos asked in a very small voice.

I pulled him around to the front windows, jiggling them to maybe find a loose latch. I didn't find one . . . but I did find Conor.

I banged on the glass. 'Conor! Let us in.' He was listening to music with brand-new headphones on. I banged harder and this time he reacted. I think he saw the movement rather than heard us – he jumped in shock, like he'd seen a ghost.

He opened the front door and I barged through, fists clenched.

'What the hell?' I pushed him in the chest – possibly the first time I'd ever pushed anyone, let alone my older cousin – then flinched, imagining what would follow, but Conor was caught off guard for once. 'Look at Jos – he's freezing,' I continued, suddenly empowered.

'Yeah, well, you nearly frightened me to death, so . . .'

'We tried knocking – you weren't paying attention. What if one of the others had come back? I mean, do you even know if they did?' I took off my glasses, which were fogging up, and wiped them on my hoody.

Jos pushed past us both and ran into the kitchen crying. I threw one last glare at Conor before running after him.

Conor had been busy. He'd clearly decided breakfast was over – the remains of a ham and cheese sandwich was evidence of that, and he'd cracked open a massive bag of tortilla chips.

He followed us in, then scraped his leftover sandwich crusts into the bin, looking guilty. 'Hey, I've not been completely useless – I brought the battery-powered heater in from the caravan so the family room's warm, I typed a few messages to a bunch of people: our next-door neighbours, my mates from home – I know there's no signal but maybe they'll send. And I packed and unpacked the dishwasher.' He pointed over his shoulder. 'And there's sandwiches and fruit in the family room. And you're welcome.'

I rubbed Jos's back to warm him up and, I hoped, comfort him. I didn't have space in my head to congratulate Conor on making lunch. I stared at the dishwasher, my hand circling Jos's back.

'Hey! Did you hear me? I said I'm not complet—'

'What was in the dishwasher?' I interrupted. Something was piecing itself together in my brain.

Conor looked at me like I was being weird. But for once, I wasn't.

'I dunno – glasses, little plates, cutlery.' He shrugged.

'Breakfast bowls? Cereal spoons?' I dashed across the kitchen and flung open the bread bin. The tear-and-share pastries were still there.

Conor shook his head. 'Nah. Just the fancy glasses everyone was drinking out of last night, and the side plates we had our cold meats on. And I guess some stuff you all used before we arrived. Coffee and tea stuff.' He nodded as if he'd figured where I was going with all this.

I tipped my head towards the door. 'Jos, why don't you go warm up in the family room. And could you grab the hand-vac and hoover up the soil I spilt? You're a star. I'll be there in a sec.' I waited until I heard the hum of the mini hoover.

'There's nothing from this morning – not in the dishwasher or in the kitchen,' I said.

'Which means they didn't have breakfast?' Conor said incredulously. He was right; that was not normal for my family. 'Maybe they went out to get some – I know what your mum's like without a cup of coffee in her.' He smiled, but it looked thin and tight. Was confident Conor losing his nerve?

'I don't think so. It's Christmas Day, remember? Nothing's open.' I told him what we'd found in the little house in Knelston: covers thrown aside, front door open letting in the freezing air. It was like they'd left suddenly. They hadn't gone on holiday; two people, two toothbrushes. I was beginning to suspect that no one in our family had even made it to bed last night. 'I'm calling it. We need to phone the police.'

Conor nodded. 'I'll do it. You tell Jos – he might not handle it.'

I left Conor dialling 999 and went to the family room to be with Jos, thinking how I wasn't sure *I* was going to handle it.

Moments later, Conor joined us in the one warm room in the house, slowly shaking his head at me. He had a seriousness in his eyes that gave me pause.

'No signal. I think you're right – the storm must

have knocked out all the phone masts as well as the power.' He waved his useless phone at us. '999 should always work; even with no signal you're supposed to be able to make an emergency call.'

I didn't ask how Conor knew that.

'Why did you call 999?' said Jos, his eyes doubling in size. 'Are we in an emergency?'

I pulled him close. 'We're just not sure what's going on, Jossy. And we can't find any adults, so they always say call for help. Well, we've sort of run out of adults, so we thought it'd be a good idea to ring the police.'

'Except we can't?' Jos said in a small voice.

'No. We can't.' I chewed my lip and Jos did the same. 'So . . . let's think about what the adults would do if they were here.'

Conor grabbed a can of beer.

'I was thinking more about keeping safe, sitting tight, staying positive,' I said, glaring at him.

Conor looked like he was brewing some sarcastic reply. But then he glanced at Jos and put the can down, before going to the kitchen and grabbing a ready-made trifle instead. 'Better?'

Jos smiled. 'Better.'

Seeing him happy, I started to breathe out . . .

Then I almost choked as a knock at the door sent my heart shooting up to my throat.

All three of us froze, and we all made the same strangled noise in our throats.

Who was it? What should we do? Fight? Flight?

And then I thought: *Mum?*

7

BOXING DAY WALK

25–26 December

Jos clearly thought it was Mum too and made to run for the door, but Conor grabbed him and held him back. I was grateful for his clear thinking, as unexpected as it was; Mum had a key. So did the rest of the family.

The doorbell rang. It played this naff version of 'Good King Wenceslas' but it never got past the first few notes as the person at the door pressed it over and over again.

Conor shook his head at Jos, putting a finger to his lips, then his gaze flicked to the wide bifold doors, and back. He scurried towards them, moving silently in his stripy socks, and clicked the lock shut.

Then he beckoned to us to follow him into the windowless hallway.

I whispered as quietly as I could to Jos. 'It might be Mum, or Dad, or someone we know, but it might not.' I decided not to expand on what I meant by that and his frightened little face told me all I needed to know. 'If it's our family they'll let us know.' Same for anyone who wanted to help us.

Conor crept to the front door, crouched low, and listened.

Another knock. This one louder and more demanding. We all jumped again at the intrusive sound and Conor looked angry with himself. I pulled Jos to the bottom stair and sat beside him, holding his hand.

'Hey! I know you're in there.' It was a man's voice and no one we knew. 'I can hear you moving around.' The door handle pumped up and down urgently. Fingers pushed through the letterbox into our private space.

I could feel Jos's heartbeat through his back.

I shook my head at Conor. Maybe the person on the other side of the door was bluffing and if we just stayed really still, really quiet—

The family room suddenly lit up and I yelled out in fright. The loudness of it filled the house and my head.

No!

It was the automatic Christmas tree lights.

Masen, you idiot!

The man at the door hammered with his fist, sounding desperate now.

Conor glared at me, then flicked his hand in the direction of the first floor. We crept up the stairs as quickly as we could and into one of the bedrooms. I silently begged Conor to come away from the window but he twitched the curtains and peered through.

Jos shivered in my arms but it wasn't with cold.

What did the man want? Was he alone? Could he get in?

I mentally scanned the house. Conor had locked the doors to the patio, and the front door was secure, I hoped. But this wasn't our house. Were the windows locked? Was there another back door? I couldn't remember! Earlier we had been desperate to find someone. Now I wished whoever had found us would just go away.

The man thumped on the door like he was beating a rhythm on a drum. 'I know you're in there,' he shouted. 'Help me! Let me in! I don't want to be like them.' Then he began swearing. Jos started to cry.

Tears welled for me, too.

Then there was a new sound, distant at first, getting louder. My brain was on the verge of giving up – I felt like it wanted to pull down its own curtains and hide and pretend none of this was happening, but there was something different about this sound. Something that said: it's going to be OK.

Barking!

It was barking. The unmistakable growl slash purposeful bark of a usually daft dog telling a stranger to get lost.

Conor threw open the window and leant out. 'Get him, Kika!' He laughed, somewhat cruelly. 'Bite his leg off, girl. Go on. It's not as good as Christmas ham but it'll do. See him off, that's a good girl!'

I joined Conor at the window, and we watched the young man running off up the path, Kika bounding a few steps after him, barking, then returning, then repeating the action as if to say *I'll come after you for real if you don't keep running*.

Then we ran to the front door, scooped up Kika in our arms and fell to the floor, laughing like clowns. One of us had returned, and if one could . . .

We slept in the caravan again. I had this glimmer of a hope – ridiculous as it was – that we'd strayed into a time loop, or a space anomaly, or a spell. That we might wake up on Christmas morning like nothing had happened and we'd get the chance to do it again. Properly this time.

Jossy murmured in his sleep, kicking the covers like he was running from something. Conor was awake a lot – he lay there silently, pretending to sleep. I knew because I wasn't sleeping either. The only one who settled was Kika, who slept by the door. Her stillness calmed me and we already knew her guard-dog skills were epic. Eventually, I fell asleep, listening to Kika snore, squeezing Mum's compass.

The next morning was cold; not snowy, like Christmas morning, but chilly enough that I could see my breath. The wind and rain had started up again too. It was definitely a different day – Boxing Day for real, and not some do-over. No second chance. No returning to a previous save point.

Conor and Jossy were already up when I woke and said to meet them in the cottage kitchen, as they left me alone in the caravan to get dressed. I was annoyed at Conor for not waking me so I could look after my little brother, but at the same time grateful for his kindness. I was glad of the extra sleep – when I wasn't dreaming about people being abducted by aliens or mysteriously disappearing.

When I went to the cottage kitchen they were tucking into bread and jam, and Jossy looked happy enough, if a bit cold.

'It smells of farts in here,' I said.

'We left the pigs in blankets out,' replied Conor.

I looked around the kitchen, eager to tuck into a sausage wrapped in bacon, even a day-old one, but I couldn't see them. Then I clocked Kika, licking her lips, and understood.

I smiled. Another thing to be grateful for – I had worried I'd forgotten how.

'Any news?' I buttered two slices of bread before turning back to see Conor shaking his head.

'We should head into the village again,' he said. 'With a plan this time. Take some food, find a map, and make more of an effort to find someone.'

'Someone nice,' said Jos.

'Yes. That guy was scary, but at least we know there are still people out there.'

It was a good idea. Maybe Conor was better at this than I'd given him credit for.

'And if we can't find anyone "nice", maybe we find a car we can use,' said Conor. 'Get the hell out of here, find some phone signal.'

Jos licked his plate. 'We checked the phones, Mase, there's no signal and still no Wi-Fi. And they're all running out of battery. There's still no power.'

I nodded firmly, which I hoped hid my deep worry. My stomach was churning so much I felt like *I'd* eaten all the pigs in blankets, but I didn't want him to know that. He could still believe that everything was going to be OK.

We did exactly as Conor suggested. We bundled up in coats and hats and stuffed our pockets with Quality Streets and salt and vinegar crisps, and

Conor found an old road map of the Gŵyr – or Gower in English – in the kitchen.

'All the grown-ups' coats are still in the cupboard under the stairs,' said Jos.

Conor and I nodded, both of us filing it under information we could do nothing about just then. All I could do was hope they had jumpers on.

We put Kika on her lead and whistled for Fran, but had no luck. Kika whined in her throat, dipping her head, but then her buddy was all but forgotten when she spied a squirrel and almost tugged my arm out of its socket.

We waited for a break in the rain, then walked the same way as before, to the end of the lane, then along the main-ish road. It almost felt like a normal Sunday walk. Birds sang, eager to be heard after the snow of the previous day, showering the ground with water droplets as they darted from tree to hedge to farm gate. Traces of snow clung in shady corners.

But once again, there was no sign of human life. No traffic, no voices.

Except . . . there *was* a sound. I stopped the others and shushed Conor from stomping his cold feet on the road.

'I can't feel my face,' he complained, as the icy wind picked up. 'I thought the storm was over.'

'Shh! Listen.' There was something – a strange cry, right on the edge of my hearing.

'It's coming from that way,' said Conor, grimacing at the muddy field to our right. 'I suppose you want to go look.'

A gap in the hedge about a metre along revealed a stile, which we clambered over. Conor grumbled, and Jos had to help him land in a patch of grass so as to not muddy his trainers too much.

I shook my head at him.

I do not understand my cousin one little bit.

A narrow, trodden path followed the hedge along the perimeter of the field, taking us closer to the sound as we walked. Conor continued muttering under his breath about sticking to his plan – heading to the village and keeping to the main road. Jossy had succumbed to silence, and held tightly to Kika's lead, pulling her back when she strained in the direction of the sound.

'It sounds like an animal,' I said. I was sure we'd all had the same thought, whether we wanted to voice it or not: that we would find Fran when we found the whimpering.

But that was not what we found.

The path widened into churned, muddy ruts – most of them solid and icy, but melting and running with brown water. A series of miniature gorges had been left by tractor tyres, fanning out from a wide wooden gate another metre or so ahead. On either side was an off-putting hedge – hawthorn perhaps, weaved with holly. Apparently not spiky enough for the farmer, though, who had added barbed wire through the wooden crossbars of the gate and up the gate posts. It was by the bottom of one of these that we saw the shoe.

At first, I assumed it was just a lost shoe. Caught in the wire, yanked off, never reclaimed. But it was in the wrong place entirely. Bright pink, shiny, with a spear of a heel covered in gems. High heels . . . on a muddy farm. Even more unsuitable than Conor's must-have trainers.

And then it moved and we all understood, even Kika, who barked, then stiffened, then whined, like she didn't know how to feel. The mewling sound wasn't an animal, not Fran, not a fox in a trap. It was what we had set out to find – a person.

8

HOMING BEACON

26 December

We all sucked in short, sharp gasps of cold winter air which pricked our senses better than a slap to the face. Kika made a low noise in her throat, and Jossy's gasp turned to a gurgle – a sound I recognized. He was stuffing fear and sadness into his body. Pushing it down so we wouldn't see. But I saw. Mum said I was good at that – seeing what was going on for other people. I just wasn't so good at seeing it in myself.

'Hello. Are you all right?' I asked, like we do, even though it was perfectly clear that the person in question was far from all right. There was no answer. 'Don't move. We'll come to you.'

As I said this, Conor was already half over the gate, minding his trainers on the wire.

I crouched beside the woman's foot, steeling myself for what I might see, but I was relieved to find she was not badly injured.

'I'm just going to check your foot,' I said and touched her ankle on the knobbly bone. It was cold. She moaned.

'Sorry. Did that hurt? It doesn't look bad. The wire is mostly caught around your shoe.' The woman flexed her foot again, as if trying to free herself, and I saw that it wasn't the wire that was the main problem. The heel was stuck in the 'V' of the crossbars of the gate. She should have easily been able to sit up, unhook the wire and flick off her shoe. Maybe she was hurt more than I thought.

I stood and leant over the fence. 'Conor?'

'Stay there, Masen.' The woman was lying on her side on the freezing ground. Conor waved his hand in front of her face and when she didn't react, a jolt of panic rushed over me and I had to talk myself down.

She's not dead – her foot is moving.

I was just on edge. She moaned again and tugged

at the gate with her foot.

'Maybe stop moving.' Conor shrugged at me, then put a hand on her shoulder. 'Can you sit up?'

The woman didn't reply. Instead, she reached out her hand and grabbed at the stubby, frostbitten grass, clawing uselessly at the mud.

As the shoe suggested, she wasn't dressed for a Boxing Day walk. I guessed she'd been at a Christmas Eve party – she was wearing all black, bar the pink shoes, with a short black jacket over a black glittery dress. Long, straight jet-black hair, matted with mud, clung to her face, covering it. Her nails were a deep shade of Christmas green. Those that weren't caked in dirt.

Fear of some unknown thing I didn't understand, that might've happened to her, rolled around in my stomach.

'Excuse me,' I said to her, over the gate. 'I'm going to try to get your foot free. It might hurt a bit so sorry about that, but maybe then you can sit up and tell us who you are and what happened.' I bobbed back down to where her foot stuck out. She was wearing thin black tights and her toes were frozen in place, keeping the shape of the pointed pink shoe. 'OK, now I'm just going to pull this wire away.' It was hooked in her tights mostly, although I did feel the pull of something more substantial. Skin. But she didn't even flinch – too numb, I figured. Only once it was done did I realize how badly my hands were shaking. I threw the shoe over the fence to Conor.

'There you go, Jos. She's free now. Let's see what else we can do to help her.'

Jos nodded, half rigid with worry, and clung to Kika's neck. Kika licked his face to make him feel better.

Conor helped the woman up as she dragged her foot through the gate. She didn't appear to acknowledge any pain and wasn't even slightly interested in her shoe, even though Conor waved it at her. And then, as if nothing had happened, and she wasn't half shoeless and soaking in a freezing muddy field, she straightened up and walked away. No limp, no pain, no sign of the injured animal she'd been moments earlier. No words of thanks or explanation, no recognition of anything at all.

'Hey!' yelled Conor. 'Where are you going? Here's your shoe.' He chucked her shoe on the ground after her. He turned back to me and Jos on the other side of the fence, his arms out in bewilderment. 'What the hell?'

'Stay here and hold Kika,' I said to Jos, and bounded over the gate. I caught up with Conor, who was strutting after the woman. He put his hands on her shoulders. 'You can at least say thank—'

I was about to scold him for his tone – this woman needed us to be kind – but his words trailed off and his face froze. I swallowed. I'd never seen my cousin look scared before.

He let go of the woman like she'd given him an electric shock, and she kept on walking.

I ran after her. 'Please stop.' I grabbed her arm, spinning her around so we were face to face. She stared right through me as if she couldn't even see me at all. Then, she turned back and moved off in the same direction as before.

But I'd seen *her*. And I'd seen what scared my tough-guy cousin so badly.

Her eyes . . . the whites were completely black and the pupils and irises were one: bright orange and pink, rippling with colour. Black threads, like thin veins, looked almost painted across her eyelids and cheeks, and her face was sickly white by comparison. I turned to Conor, who looked about the same colour as the leaden sky. 'Was she . . .' I couldn't finish but Conor found the words for me.

'Infected.' He leant over and vomited.

9

CONTAGIOUS

26 December

Jos was bobbing up and down on the gate, his feet wide to avoid the barbed wire. 'What's going on?'

'Stay there, Jossy,' I called, grimacing at Conor, who was spitting into the grass. 'What do you mean, infected? You think she was sick?'

Conor wiped his mouth with his sleeve. 'Yeah – sick. Like people get bloodshot eyes when they're properly poorly and her eyes were . . .'

'Blackshot?' I suggested.

And not just her eyes . . . her skin too.

'Yeah – not normal. And look at her go. Infected *and* possessed – like a zombie.' He started pacing about. 'That's what's happened to everyone. They're freaking zombies.'

'Don't say that, Conor. That's not a thing.' My voice got higher as he paced and my certainty got lower. Was this all related to our family going missing? Had they turned into zombies? The woman looked every bit like a zombie. Except . . .

'She didn't want to eat us, though, so maybe it's something else. Not a zombie thing.' I cast an unhappy glance at the discarded pink shoe and walked back to the gate.

What now?

'What now, Mase?' said Jos, reading my mind.

I helped him over the fence and into the field, as Kika found a safe route through the hedge. She sniffed the shoe, growled, then backed away, cowering.

'Should we go after her?' I said to Conor. 'She didn't really seem like she wanted our help.'

'But maybe she's poorly,' said Jos. 'She doesn't look right.'

Of course Jos wanted to help. He was such a kind thing. 'I know, but she's a grown-up, right? And we're just kids. She can't expect us to chase after her if she won't even talk to us.' I didn't want to mention her eyes or her dead-looking skin.

'The best thing is to carry on to the village. Then we can get help for us, and her,' said Conor, being all sensible and capable again.

'Where is she going, do you think? She seemed very determined,' I said.

'She's going to the coast,' called a voice from behind the hedge.

I jumped out of my skin. I grabbed Jos and spun around towards the sound, where I locked eyes with a girl. Slightly older than me, I thought, with black corkscrew curls stuffed into a red woolly hat and a thick scarf that almost obscured her face. She pointed. 'That way.' She jogged to the gate, lifted the metal latch and heaved it open just enough to squeeze through. She stomped towards us in sensible blue wellies, one mittened hand extended. 'Hi, I'm Gloria. Are you OK? Was that your first?'

'Our first . . . what do you mean?' I shook Gloria's hand, a most formal greeting for our situation.

'First person who's um . . .' She seemed to be looking for a description, maybe one that wasn't zombie. 'Affected.'

'Affected by what?' Conor inserted himself between us as the older one in charge.

'You know, with the . . .' She pointed at her eyes and turned in the direction of the not-zombie woman, just stumbling over the hill.

Wait . . . is this all connected? Terrible, awful thoughts sent a chill down my spine, like a snowball had been shoved down the back of my jumper.

Is my whole family like . . . that?

Not zombies, NOT zombies.

Affected?

The world went out of focus and I thought I might pass out.

Gloria put a hand on my shoulder to steady me. 'Are you alone?' she asked.

Jos nodded. 'They all disappeared,' he said. 'Our mum, our dad, our uncles, aunty. Nanny Sasha, too. And one of the dogs.' Kika barked. I didn't know which one of the list tipped Jos over the edge, but he fell to a crouch on the ground and sobbed. I took off my glasses to wipe away my own tears and smiled weakly at Gloria, grateful that someone was here who seemed to have answers.

She put a padded arm around Jossy's shoulders.

'I'm sorry, peanut.' She sniffed and plucked off a glove to wipe her eyes. 'Oh look, you've gone and got me going now too. It's contagious!' She rubbed Jos's back vigorously. 'But not everyone's gone. And they're not *gone*, gone. They're just sick. My dad says they'll get well again, don't you worry.'

So, I was right. 'Are you saying that our family have been affected . . . infected?' I said.

'Will we catch it too?' asked Jos.

'And they *will* get better?' said Conor, almost as if he hadn't even entertained the possibility that things would be OK again.

Gloria was patient as we flooded her with questions. 'Probably your family have got it – it mostly affects adults. So, no, you shouldn't catch it. And sure – I think they'll all be much better soon. Come on, I'll take you to him – Dad, that is. He's helping to get people to safety, especially the kids. There's a place you can go and be looked after until it's all over.' Gloria stood, held her hand out to Jossy and pulled him up. 'Don't you worry, peanut. Everything's going to be just fine, you'll see.'

They led, Jos telling her all about our so-called Christmas, and we followed, walking in the same direction as the woman with one pink shoe.

Crows startled from their perches as we passed, scolding us for disturbing them. I watched their flight, from the bare trees into the grey of the afternoon. We were the only sound in the silence and it made me want to shout. I usually preferred the quiet but this had such an end-of-days feel to it that it made my body tight and my bones brittle, and I just wanted to curl into a ball and hide in the hedgerow.

'How far is the safe place?' I asked Gloria.

'About a mile,' she called over her shoulder. 'Just over this ridge here is an old ruined castle. We'll have to climb over the wall but on the other side, you'll see the sea.'

I wondered if she thought we'd be excited by this prospect. Like we were on holiday. And then I remembered. We *were* supposed to be on holiday. We should be playing a Boxing Day board game right now.

Kika barked and I let her off the lead for a run around. She found the tumbledown old castle and the wall first, marking it with her scent for other dogs to read. Mum said that dogs wee on things like it's their social media. Maybe Kika had left a notification for Fran.

We clambered over the wall, pushing aside bare branches and spiky firs and if you can believe it, I saw the sea and I *was* a little bit thrilled. A patch of blue was layered over the horizon where sea met sky, and a large, low boat seemed to hover in that in-between space, a light winking at us from a distance.

But below that was something my mind couldn't quite grasp.

We hadn't had the chance to go down to the beach on our so-called Christmas holiday, so I didn't know what it would otherwise look like, but it wouldn't be this. I couldn't see if it was sand or shingle because it was crammed with people. It might have looked like a beach festival, except for the sound coming up on the breeze. It sent a chill through me that had nothing to do with the weather.

It was the same animal moaning that the woman in the field had made – desperate and desolate, but amplified a hundred times.

One hundred people. One hundred *Infected*.

10

THEY DO LIKE TO BE BESIDE THE SEASIDE

26 December

Gloria grabbed me, yanking me away from the scene. I didn't know how long I'd been staring at the moaning mass of people on the beach.

'What are they doing?'

I loved Jos in that moment for his directness. He asked the big questions in his sweet, small way.

Gloria turned him away from the view too, spinning him slowly by the shoulders. 'They're trying to keep warm by heading south, like birds in the winter. They've come from the local area, and they've all ended up here, jostling like that.'

Jos's eyes were wide and brimming with tears.

Gloria swept him into a hug, enveloping him in her warm, soft coat. 'Don't worry, peanut, they're fine. They're not in danger. They push and shove, wanting to keep walking, and then, when they sense how cold the sea is, they try and get out again. They're like the tide, ebbing and flowing, pushing and pulling. One of my dad's team is keeping an eye on them until they can get rescued.'

When Gloria put it like that it didn't sound too bad.

'I don't understand. Are they . . . zombies?' said Jos.

'If they are, they're the worst zombies I've ever seen.' Conor was still staring out to sea. 'Zombies that want fish brains,' he scoffed. 'They look so slow even you could get away, Mase.'

I tried to ignore him – he was just showing off, being 'brave', but he knew how to sting me. Pretending not to care, I whistled for Kika, who was racing around the field sniffing for messages. Like a coward, I waited for Jos to ask the question we really needed to ask.

'Are our family down there? Mum and Dad?'

Gloria took his hand. 'You said you were staying

in the farmhouse just outside Knelston? Well, that's close, so they would've got here quickly and would have been some of the first ones to be rescued. If you're lucky they'll already be in hospital being looked after.'

Jossy's eyes lit up and he wiped away what was left of his windblown tears.

'What's wrong with them? Why are they like that?' I asked. 'And how do they get better?'

Gloria frowned like she was looking for the answer in her shoes. 'I . . . it's complicated – something to do with . . . no, it's better if my dad explains it. All I know is a bunch of people have already been taken to hospital in Swansea for treatment, but because it's Christmas everything's a bit slow and there's a lot of people affected. That's why Dad's team is monitoring them and scooping up all the unaffected kids. But there's nothing to worry about. Not really.'

'Nothing to worry about' was reassuring.

'Not really' was not.

We followed Gloria along a rough, worn path towards the sand dunes that lay between us and the beach, up through prickly gorse and seagrass. The ground grew increasingly sandy and on steeper parts wooden slats appeared beneath our feet, there, I guessed, to keep the path from drifting away. We slipped frequently – the combination of sand and what was left of the snow was lethal. I held tight to Jos, although it might have been better to let him fall given the number of times I almost yanked his arm from its socket as he lost his footing. Kika ran on ahead, sure-footed and swift.

As we climbed the dune, no one spoke. We just watched our feet, and the weird coastal foliage, thistly and rough. Shells poked through the sand, along with sea glass and rocks worn smooth by time. And all the time the moaning, like the mournful wail of ghosts, came in with the sea breeze.

Halfway up the dune, Gloria took a right along a steep, narrow, unkept path that cut across the slope rather than going straight up it. I was glad that we weren't heading directly for the beach any more. The grass here was taller and rapier-sharp, like swaying swords. Conor grabbed a handful and tried to pull it out but only managed to slice his palm. He wiped the blood on his shorts, flecks spattering his legs.

'Where are we going?' I asked as we blindly followed Gloria through the grass.

'There's a campsite over the crest of this dune. Dad should be there . . .'

I thought she would say more but she stopped and held her hands out flat beside her, running her fingers lightly over the grass. I watched her, mesmerized, then copied her. I don't know why – she just looked so serene, but I quickly realized what she was doing. The grass was vibrating. Shuddering, like it would in the wind . . . if the wind were coming from below.

'What *is* that?' I asked.

All around, the dune grass shimmered and rippled and Gloria's expression turned from one of curious patience to urgency. 'We need to pick up the pace.'

Then I saw why. I stood motionless for a beat, my brain still processing what I was seeing: heads bobbing above the grass behind us, at the bottom of the slope we'd just climbed. Hundreds of them. Maybe even more than were on the beach. I squeezed Jos's hand and we walked faster.

Conor was right behind us, out of breath and slipping on the sand. The path was narrow and restrictive. He whistled for Kika but she was nowhere to be seen.

'Wait up. What's the rush? They're just people,' shouted Conor.

They were just people . . . but a wall of them, pushing through the grass towards us, from the direction of the main road. They were walking, not charging, but they were fast and forceful – determined to keep moving towards the beach, like the one-shoed woman. They were also getting closer all the time, because while we were heading roughly parallel to the sea, they were heading straight for it! I thought about what Gloria had said about the infection only affecting adults. That we *probably* wouldn't catch it.

'I thought you said they weren't scary!' yelled Jos.

'They aren't,' replied Gloria from the front of our stumbling line. 'But I don't like the look of this. They're like a herd of animals.'

'Why are there so many all of a sudden, all arriving together?' yelled Conor.

Gloria started running, yelling over her shoulder. 'Maybe they're gathering together for body heat, 'cause it's so cold.'

'So they could sense our heat too?' I said.

I felt Jos speed up.

The infected people marched steadily but unrelentingly closer.

'We're not going to make it past the edge of the herd if we stay on this path. We need to run in front of them, in the same direction as them. They're slow, we're not. We can stay ahead,' barked Conor.

'No! Stick to the path,' shouted Gloria. 'The ground is unsteady on the dunes. You'll end up in a hole, twist your ankle, and they'll be on you. They won't walk around you!' Gloria waved her arm above her head. 'Come on!'

Conor was about to complain but then one of the infected people closest to us suddenly dropped from sight, crumpling to the ground in front of the crowd, swallowed by sand and grass. Just like Gloria said, the others kept coming and I watched in horror as the herd of people rose up above the grass and then went back down, like they were cresting a wave. They were walking over the person who fell. I heard a sound like a snapping twig and tried to pretend that was all it was.

We ran faster, the herd gaining on us with every pace. Another Infected fell beside me, before reaching through the grass to grab at my leg. I screamed and kicked them off, feeling sick with disgust at myself.

We should be saving them!

But I couldn't. More were coming; they tripped over the body, grasping for it, attracted to its warmth, but mine too. Hands reached for me, grazing my shoulder, touching my hair, before dropping away as they fell over the fallen person, piling up for more to follow. A mound of bodies grew in the grass like a molehill, the person at the bottom of the heap now obscured from view, crushed, maybe suffocating – and still, Gloria led us on. I loped across the dune, staggering on a root, and this time it was Jossy who pulled me back to my feet. 'Come on, Mase – look, Gloria's safely through.'

He was right. I clambered up and exploded out of the grass into clear space, and only then did I look back for Conor.

He was gone.

11

ANOTHER CARAVAN

26 December

'CONOR!' I was sure he'd been right behind me.

Gloria took Jossy's hand, that urgent look on her face again telling me to follow her, but I couldn't leave Conor to be crushed to death. The herd of infected people was still moving ever on towards the sea, but I spotted a gap and jumped back on to the path, sweeping the grass aside left and right. I swore as I caught my skin on the sharp edges.

'Find him, Mase!' yelled Jos. 'Can you see him?'

I didn't stop to consciously consider why I was risking my life for my cousin, but I knew deep down it was more about Jos than doing the right thing by Conor. I figured I'd feel bad about *that* later.

'I think I see him,' I yelled. He was right on the edge of the danger zone, cowering behind a solid lump of dune sand and grass which was funnelling the herd around him, and thank God for those ridiculous socks of his – white and red stripes gleaming in all the yellow. I always thought he was so daft wearing shorts, even in winter, just to show off how tough he was, but maybe it had just saved him. I ploughed towards him, diving down to grab his hand as he was pushing himself up. He slapped my hand away.

'I'm fine,' he said. But I could see he wasn't. He'd gone over in one of the holes Gloria had warned us about and hit his head on a large, smooth rock, half buried in the sand. His hair was sticky with blood; sand stuck to it like on a dropped toffee apple. I couldn't hide my grimace.

An Infected suddenly fell against the lump of dune, flopping over it and almost landing in Conor's lap. It reached for him, grabbing his hair and he cried out, stumbling away and clutching his ankle as he went down on one knee. This time he didn't fight when I took his hand and pulled him up. An Infected pushed past me on the left, then the right and suddenly they were all around us. It wasn't like being in a crowd of kids. These people were strong, tall adults, all striding purposefully ahead. We staggered with them, taken by the current as if we were being swept out to sea. My glasses threatened to fall off my face. I could see Jos through the crowd, still with Gloria, hopping up and down, waving, shouting.

I pulled Conor's arm around my shoulder and together we barged through the swarm of bodies, ducking under armpits, pushing aside chests, in the direction of Gloria and Jos. Conor stumbled again, a cry of pain spitting out between gritted teeth. Adults surrounded us, wearing suits and dresses, one in a Santa costume, one in Christmas reindeer pyjamas. Tall people, short people, people with ponytails, beards, glasses, jewellery. All with the same greying skin, streaked with black inky patterns and . . . I avoided their eyes.

I couldn't see Jos any more; I couldn't see anything, apart from the people pressing into me and Conor from all sides, closer and tighter. They smelt sweaty and hot and there was something else, something like mouldy bread and cheap air freshener.

Conor was heavy. I was going to have to stop, just for a minute, catch my breath. I slowed, and a tall woman buffeted into me. I staggered into the back of someone else. My legs buckled . . . and then, light and air reached us again and there was Gloria, shoving through the throng, knocking the infected people forcibly aside with her elbows and . . .

Thwack!

An Infected went down at the knees beside me. Another thudding sound followed and a black-eyed woman in a cat onesie folded over behind Gloria and fell backwards into an old man in an elf hat. They started going down like dominoes, long enough for me to drag Conor into the gap they left and back out of the dunes.

Sucking in cold fresh air, I hitched Conor up to a more comfortable position and saw Gloria standing, triumphantly, a small plastic kayak oar in her hand.

'Thanks,' I croaked.

'You're welcome. Come on, I've found us a caravan that's unlocked. There's more coming.' She tipped her head, both to a row of brown, fake-wood static caravans and beyond, to another arm of the infected herd, coming through the wide driveway on to the site.

How have so many arrived here all at once?

I glanced back to take in the sheer scale of Infected moving towards the beach and saw a growing pile-up of bodies, an elf hat lying beside them on the sand.

They'll be fine though. Once they get to hospital.

I knew it wasn't true.

Gloria swung open the door to the holiday caravan. Jos was already in and . . .

Kika!

I covered her in hugs and scratches and wet tears. Conor was crying too. I didn't know he could.

Gloria kicked the door closed and turned the small latch. It was little more than something you'd get on a toilet door. All that stood between us and the Infected. I ran to the back and pulled open the short, ugly curtains. People were streaming on to the site – most of them instinctively navigated around the caravans, cars and RVs, but not all. One Infected was stuck over the boot of a car, legs still pumping but going nowhere. It should've been hilarious. It wasn't.

Gloria rummaged through the cupboards and found some paracetamol and a can of Fanta. She handed them to Conor, who took them without a word. I could tell he was trying not to puke – he'd gone whiter than his once-perfect trainers . . . ruined, of course, after the dunes.

'We'll be safe in here,' said Gloria. It annoyed me how Jos calmed down at the sound of her voice, her reassurance, rather than mine. I sat beside him on the floor and smoothed his hair.

'Anything to eat in there?' I asked.

Gloria laughed. 'Guess you're OK if you can think of your stomach,' she said, chucking me a mini tube of Pringles and a box of Celebrations.

'It's not for me,' I said, annoyed that she'd made me explain myself. I made a point of handing them to Jos.

'Sure,' she said, still laughing as I glowered at her. I don't know why I was mad – she saved us, after all.

I called Kika over, patting my thighs, and she sat between my legs so I could pick out the many burrs she'd gathered in her fur.

'So, we wait for your dad?' I asked.

‘We wait until it’s safe to leave,’ said Gloria.

‘How come your dad isn’t infected?’ Jos said after inhaling half the Pringles.

‘Jos!’ I spat out a mini Mars. ‘That’s rude!’ Then I wasn’t sure. ‘Is it rude?’

Gloria looked like she was considering it. Then she sat down and said, ‘Not at all. No, none of us were infected.’ Her leg jiggled. ‘I don’t know why.’

A theory popped into my mind, brought on by the smell of the infected people. ‘We had these odd plants in our cottage – mini Christmas trees, with mushroom-like flowers growing out of them. They almost looked fake, like they’d been stuck on. They all died suddenly and I wondered . . . could they have something to do with this? Could they be toxic? I can’t explain why the plants died, though. At first, I thought it was the cold, but I’m not sure.’

She nodded. ‘I saw some people in the village with those little trees. They looked weird. And some plants are definitely poisonous . . . You might be on to something. We didn’t have them either – we had holly and ivy – Dad’s more into traditional stuff. A Christmas tree, of course. Laurel and winter jasmine, and seed pods like teasels, poppy and nigella . . . I take after Dad I'm afraid – a plant nerd.'

Had I been looking at her weirdly? I wasn't sure, but I guess I had been for her to explain herself like that.

Conor swung his bad leg up on to what passed for a sofa. 'So what's a pair of plant nerds doing in the middle of all this? And what about the rest of your family?'

'No other family here, just me and Dad. And the reason we're mixed up in this is that there's not exactly anyone else. This is a small community – we don't stand around while people need help. Dad's really well known around here and . . . well, we might be the only people not infected by this . . . *thing*. He says we should do what we can until help can reach us. According to Dad, all the roads out of Gŵyr are blocked after the storm – mostly fallen trees, but a car accident too.'

Conor looked at her in disbelief.

'They're rural roads – this isn't Cardiff,' she said. 'And there's no one to clear the blockages.'

Gloria steadied herself as the caravan wobbled, jostled by infected people as they flowed past. We ducked out of sight and watched their shadows through the thin curtains, and waited for the flood of bodies to pass.

12

TAKING THE PLUNGE

26 December

I woke as the sun was almost setting, the comfort of a dream about Christmas dinner and party games drifting away. Conor was asleep under a blanket and the Infected seemed to have passed us by. At least, the shadows had gone and the caravan was still. Gloria and Jos were in the middle of a game of whisper-Dobble on the tiny caravan table, lit by the light of a camping lantern, and Jossy looked almost happy.

He saw me and slammed his card on the pile in the centre, yelling 'GHOST!' Then he slid off his seat and threw himself into a me-hug. It was warm and just a tiny bit sweaty. Kika ran around in circles looking for whatever Jossy had been shouting at.

Gloria put her fingers to her lips. 'Shh, poppet.'

Is she shushing because of Conor, or the Infected?

I wasn't sure if loud noises would attract them . . . I didn't want to find out.

I patted Kika to calm her down and willed my sleep-fuzzed brain into action.

Jos was my responsibility, and with Conor asleep and Gloria sitting there looking all calm and OK about everything, my mind raced as to what we should do next. Go back to the cottage, have a shower (maybe cold), make some food (definitely cold), and maybe look for Fran while we hid and waited for everyone to get well? Or go with Gloria to meet her dad and go to this refuge she mentioned. I thought of the man knocking on the cottage door, trying to get in, and my decision was all but made.

As if reading my thoughts, Gloria packed up the cards and said, 'He's way too good at that game.' She smiled at Jos. 'I'd forgotten how much fun it is.'

'Yeah, we only ever play it on holiday,' I said, thinking how we should be playing it right now with the rest of our family.

'We've got lots of games at Dad's place,' said

Gloria. 'There are already a bunch of kids there, all ages, and did I tell you about Dafydd, and Lily and her sons? They run the house. It's good, I promise. Safe.'

Going with her probably wasn't a bad idea. We could use some adult help – although Conor would probably disagree with that. But Jos deserved to be properly looked after and I wasn't sure I was doing a good enough job.

Keen to be on the move, now that I'd made a decision, I shook Conor awake. He groaned, either with disapproval or discomfort, I couldn't tell, and I felt a bit bad. Gloria and I had cleaned his head wound and stuck on a plaster from the small first aid kit, but the bruise had already bloomed enough to be angrily visible around the edges. Maybe I should've let him sleep a bit longer.

As Conor adjusted to the room, to the circumstances, to the pain, Gloria helped Jos into his coat and stuffed the Dobble in his pocket. 'Rematch later, right?'

I grabbed the lantern and turned it off so I could see better through the small window that overlooked the 'road'.

‘All clear.’ I unlatched the door and was barely down the little metal steps when I saw someone lying on the grass beside the caravan opposite.

‘Hello?’ I said quietly. Kika whined.

Behind me, the others stopped, waiting, breath-holding, but the person didn’t move.

‘We should help them,’ I said, although to my horror I realized that I didn’t mean it. I didn’t think we could and I didn’t know what to do to help anyway.

Gloria put a hand on my shoulder. ‘Come on. We can tell Dad they’re here and he’ll know what to do.’

We moved off in silence, Gloria repeatedly looking over her shoulder at the body. We passed empty caravans, some with their doors open, some with crayon drawings of Santas and wonky snowmen Blu-Tacked on the inside. We saw dead mushroom-trees in the windows.

As we ran the last few metres of the path to the campsite entrance, the freezing rain returned.

Gloria led the way around a sweeping bend from the static caravans, past the little shop and reception and on to a large, empty field that I guessed was usually the camping area. Kika ran in bigger circles now, barking at the rain.

Despite everything we'd been through, Jos tugged on my arm as we passed the giant footballs and crabbing buckets, fishing nets and bodyboards hanging outside the shop.

'We can't buy stuff, Jossy. The shop isn't open.' I hurried him past and caught up with Gloria, who was looking around, worry creased across her forehead.

'Dad said he'd pick us up here.'

We all did that thing of looking around even though we didn't know who or what we were looking for. Kika aimed her barking towards the next field.

'Shh, Kika. It's just another field. The grass over there is not greener.' I fussed her and she quieted for a moment but then started barking again even more insistently. 'What is it, girl? Can you hear something?'

Conor grumbled that all he could hear was his stomach rumbling and his head throbbing but then I heard it, and Gloria looked like she had too – a strange whizzing, whirring sound.

She raced off and Jos made to dash after her, but

I stopped him. 'Stay here. Conor?'

Conor glared. 'Go ahead. Run after your girlfriend. I'll babysit.' He sat down on the shop step, out of the rain, rubbing his ankle.

Ugh. Why are you so annoying?

I wanted to shake Conor for being so selfish, but Gloria had already reached the second camping field.

'She's not my girlfriend,' I hissed as I ran after her along the tarmac, wiping the drizzle from my glasses. The wind had picked up and to my left, I could hear the sea churning in the dark. I caught up to Gloria as she went through the kissing gate at the end of the path. In my haste I got jammed, like when you don't walk through ticket gates quickly enough. I hoped she hadn't seen, as I freed myself and caught up to her on top of a grassy ridge.

Below us was another beach, this one piled with rocks and smooth stones. Oily water lapped at the shoreline, which was a tangle of seaweed and rubbish – bottles and plastic mostly. A smell worked its way up to me, something like rotting seafood and burnt rubber.

The oily beach lined a narrow cove – a U-shape

guarded to our right by a steep, scrubby cliff. Mum had said something about smugglers using the coves around here hundreds of years ago, and she'd planned a fun hike for the day after Boxing Day.

Tomorrow!

A path cut its way up the cliff, through prickly gorse and heather, splitting off now and then. It seemed tiny in the distance and reminded me of a marble run. I suddenly realized what Kika had been barking at.

What did you think *you'd see, Mase?*

People. I guessed about two hundred were in clear view and I figured there were more behind, obscured by trees and the headland dipping back and away.

So many people.

The herd we'd seen had not gone directly south. Perhaps their autopilot had gone wrong but somehow they'd ended up . . . up there.

They seemed to sway in the breeze like the dune grass, hesitant, waiting. They weren't moaning like the ones on the beach – a fact I should've been grateful for but wasn't. Somehow, the heavy, empty silence was worse. Perhaps if they'd been making a horrible noise, I would've looked away sooner and not seen . . . but I couldn't stop staring.

And so I saw.

It happened so fast and yet, at the same time, in slow motion. The person closest to the edge shivered in the wind like a sliver of dune grass, then silently slid off the edge of the cliff.

13

ANOTHER ONE MISSING

26 December

A sound pierced my eardrums, a clattering noise that drowned out everything else in my brain, and it took me a moment to realize it was Gloria screaming. It could just as easily have been me.

I think I knew that more people had followed, going over the cliff edge to slide into the grim, oily sea below. And what if they hit the rocks? But I'd had the sense to look away quickly. I hoped Gloria had too because once you saw something like that you could never unsee it, and I was grateful for the cloudy twilight that saved us from seeing too much.

Still, my imagination was determined to fill in the gaps and I turned away from Gloria and her time-slowing scream and vomited Pringles into the grass.

I wiped my mouth with my sleeve and fell slowly backwards to sit on the sloping bank, where the tears came, hard and steady. Gloria crouched beside me and I could feel her shaking.

So we both leapt out of our skins as a loud Welsh voice boomed from the crest of the hill.

'Gloria!'

Gloria shot to her feet and ran to the man, who buried her in a bearded bear hug. 'Dad!'

'Bloody Nora, come away from here right now. You don't need to see this,' said the man.

'Dad, I found . . . some friends. This is Masen. We left Conor and Jos at the campsite reception.' She sobbed into her dad's thick waterproof coat. 'This is . . . awful, Dad.'

The man held her by the shoulders. 'I know. I'm sorry, love.' He looked over at me and beckoned. 'Come on, come away. I've got the car. Lily and her boys are dealing with it.' He looked up at the cliff, shaking his head. 'Somehow the Infected got diverted by a couple of fallen trees, followed the hedgerows and ended up there. It's very unfortunate.'

He rubbed his forehead and looked pained. 'We're stopping them, now.'

The whirring we'd heard before got suddenly louder and closer and a shape in my peripheral vision caught my eye. I risked a look – it was a drone. A thin rope was attached to it which a woman on the far end of the cliff grabbed. The other end was held by a man, and together they used the rope to guide the people away from the cliff edge.

Gloria grabbed my arm. 'Come on,' she said, pulling me up. 'Dad's right. We shouldn't be here. There's nothing we can do.' Pain flashed in her eyes and I understood it – frustration and helplessness in the face of something so simple.

A gull screeched across the cove, a harsh, unfriendly sound.

Gloria was pulling me but I resisted. 'There must be something?'

'There is,' she said. 'We can make sure Conor and Jos are OK. He'll be worried, your little brother.'

I don't think she meant it to sting but it did. Was she suggesting I didn't have his best interests at heart? He was my brother and I knew what was right for him.

'He's fine. Conor is family, he'll take care of him.' I turned away from the cliff and strode back towards the empty camping fields, speeding up as I went. Jos would be fine. Absolutely.

Thoughts whirred in me like the drone blades but they all flew away the instant I saw Jos, huddled in the reception doorway. Alone.

'That little . . . TURD!' I would have said something worse if Jos hadn't been there. 'We were only gone a few minutes. What is his problem?' Kika woofed as if she wanted to know the answer to this too.

'Guess his ankle wasn't so bad then?' Gloria's eyebrow twitched.

'Conor heard motorbikes on the road over there and went to see if it was people come to help us,' said Jos. 'I said it was dangerous but he laughed at me and told me to sit tight. He said he'd get me something from the shops, but I thought you said all the shops were shut.'

My heart broke at Jos's innocence. 'They are. He'll be back soon enough once he realizes that.' I flashed Gloria a warning look but I knew she wouldn't say anything to scare Jos. Even though she'd made me feel like a bad brother, I was glad she was here. She was better than Conor any day.

She turned to Jos. 'Maybe it would be OK if you borrowed one of the big footballs from the campsite reception just for a little while. I know it's dark, but we could have a kick around for a minute . . . play silent-footie while Mase goes to tell Conor we're ready to leave.'

My heart stuttered as Jos's face broke into the most joyful smile and he ran off towards the balls, bobbing in the breeze.

Once he was out of earshot, Gloria said, 'I'm pretty sure I know who Conor went off with and they are *not* here to help. This is a small village out of season, and there aren't that many ear-splitting, earth-shaking dirt bikes that could wake the . . .'

Dead.

'Anyway, I think you should find Conor and tell him to come to the safe house with us. We shouldn't leave anyone behind.'

Tell Conor what to do? *Tell* him to come with us? Not likely. I swallowed down my shame and said, 'He'll be fine.'

Coward.

'I don't know, Masen. Think about what we just saw. It's not safe out there. For anyone. I don't just mean those bikers . . . or the Infected. What if things start falling apart? People, I mean. There's no police around, there's no power. People get angry, dangerous. I don't know you all that well, but I don't like to think of Conor with . . . well, they're not nice people.'

Once again, I thought of the man at the cottage trying to get in.

'Why don't you go?' As soon as I said it, I felt childish. Why should Gloria go? She wasn't family and as she'd just pointed out, we hardly knew each other. 'Or . . . we could tell the people at the safe house there's a Conor Haarket in the village and someone can come get him?'

Gloria was beginning to look irritated. 'That's what Dad and I are doing. Finding people. We found you, now we need to go. Dad won't be impressed if we've lost someone already.'

Jos returned to us, the giant foam ball in his arms so all I could see of him was his head and legs.

'Are we playing, then?' he asked.

Gloria's expression shifted into a wide smile. 'Yes! As long as we're quiet. We don't want to draw attention to ourselves . . . from anyone.'

'Mase, you playing?'

Gloria turned to me. 'No, Mase is going to get Conor. Aren't you?'

14

END OF THE WORLD PIT STOP

26 December

Furious, I left the campsite and stomped along the road towards the shops. The rain had stopped but now the wind was hurling sand at me instead.

I could hardly believe that Gloria had said that in front of Jos. And then Jos had beamed and called me brave, so I'd had no other choice. And now here I was, alone in the near-dark, straining to listen for sounds of Infected, or movement, or arms reaching out to me . . .

Stop!

A herring gull sang out in the cloudy sky and the sea breeze brought the smell of salt. I took a long, deep breath and counted to ten to recentre myself.

I let my shoulders drop. It was only a two-minute walk to the shops where Gloria said I might find Conor. I could do this. I would be OK.

I'll be angry at Gloria later.

At the end of the road was a roundabout which joined the single road from the village. I crossed to the other side, sat on a bench and cried into my hands. What if I wasn't OK? What if things were never OK again?

Seeing those people on the cliff . . . it was the most awful thing I had ever experienced. And the thought that Mum and Dad could be up there, the uncles, and Suzie and Nanny Sasha.

Would Nanny Sasha have even survived the infection?

It was too much.

I tried to picture them in hospital, safe already, but my brain kept seeing Mum's face on the woman in the field, staggering off with her pink shoe in one hand. With the roads impassable, how could they be safe?

Mum's compass was still in my pocket and I got it out and smoothed my thumb over the glass. I was facing west; the sun was all but gone now over the horizon, but there was still a glow. I wiped my nose on my sleeve and stood up straight.

One step at a time, right, Mum?

Thinking of the others in hospital made me wonder how badly Conor was actually injured. Perhaps his knock to the head meant he wasn't thinking straight . . . maybe he wasn't doing this to be a pain in the backside and he needed me.

Find Conor, get to the safe house, then wait to be rescued.

A step-by-step plan.

I turned towards the shops facing the beach – a gift shop, two chippies and two ice cream shops. My mouth watered even though the lights were off and the shutters down.

The side window of one of the fish and chip shops had been smashed and as I peered in I saw the place was a total mess. Looters had smashed everything. I wondered if someone might be inside, in need of help, but at the same time I was terrified that there *would* be someone inside. I didn't exactly know what to do with an Infected if I found one.

A roar from the road behind the shop made me

jump backwards, crunching broken glass under my shoes. It sounded like some kind of terrifying beast, but then my brain got its act together – it was a motorbike.

Conor!

I steeled myself for confrontation, never my strong point, and headed as confidently as I could towards the sound.

As I turned the corner, voices carried on the air, jokey and carefree, as if it were a summer's day by the seaside. I hesitated, then carried on again, not sure if it was confidence driving me or the humiliation of telling Gloria I couldn't even face my own cousin.

I found him sitting on a picnic table outside a pub called the Ship.

'Masen? What the hell?' Conor's face lit up in a blush that faded as quickly as a firework.

'What are you doing, Con?'

'None of your beeswax.' He looked like he was chilling out on his holidays, leaning back on his hands, a finger disappearing into the hole in the centre of the table where an umbrella would fit on a sunnier day.

'Gloria said you should come back,' I said, sounding a little pathetic.

'Gloria can go and—'

'Oi, oi! What's this then?' A new voice cut off Conor. 'New recruits to the cause?'

I bit my lip, not wanting anything to do with this new person. She was older than both of us and perhaps the owner of the bike, dressed in thick denim and a leather jacket. Her arm was wearing a deep-green helmet like a bracelet.

'This is my little cousin, Masen. Mase, don't be rude. Say hello.'

'Hello.'

The young woman laughed from deep in her throat. 'Well isn't it just lovely to meet you, Masen. You joining us?'

Conor scowled. 'No, he's not.'

I wished with all my being that I could just teleport home immediately. 'Gloria's dad is waiting to take us to the safe house.'

Biker-girl poked her tongue around in her cheek. 'Maybe you should run along, Conor – you wouldn't want to keep the good doctor waiting.'

Conor smirked, but he looked suddenly much

younger than her, and the bruise on his head looked sore and black.

'No? Well in that case . . .' In a fluid move, she laced her arm through mine and dragged me into the pub.

It was a big place, with a wide dining area to the right and a more cosy snug room to the left. Someone had broken a glass right by the front door.

Biker-girl held the snug door open for us both. 'Table for four, is it? I think we can fit you in.'

The pub smelt of old beer and furniture polish and a smoky fire in the hearth. An older lad, also in leathers, was chucking random stuff on to it but it wasn't taking very well – wooden spoons and napkins and tea towels were smouldering, stubbornly refusing to light. 'Bloody hell, Alys, who's this now? I thought we were laying low?'

'He's Conor's cuz. And he wants a drink, don't you, mini-Conor?' She leapt over the bar and disappeared from view, popping back up again a second later with beer bottles laced into her fingers. One for each of us. Then she reached below the counter and grabbed a baseball bat. 'Hey, we could play on the beach. If it wasn't so crowded!' She laughed and I felt sick to my stomach.

'Look, I told Gloria I'd tell you,' I said to Conor, 'and now I've told you. So I'll be off.'

The girl . . . Alys, leant on her elbows. 'Back to Gloria? Your girlfriend, is she?'

'No.'

Alys studied me. 'Are you sure?' She snatched a couple of packets of crisps from a box above her head. 'You don't have to go with her, you know. You can stay here. Free drinks, free snacks. No tunes but eventually the power will come back on.'

We sat around a table, like a family out for Sunday lunch. Except I couldn't stop my legs jiggling.

'Drink up, little lad,' said Alys, putting a bottle of beer in front of me.

She must know I'm not old enough to drink.

I slid down in my seat, heart hammering. Could she tell I was sweating? Alys slung her arm around my shoulder, pulling me close and tight, her leather jacket creaking. The woody smell of it collided with a sweet, flowery perfume. I wished she would leave me alone.

Instead, she grabbed an expensive-looking camera from her backpack.

'Say cheese,' she said, taking my picture.

'Alys, don't tease the boy. This isn't some uni project of yours, this is serious,' said the big lad, giving up on the fire. He stood up, tall and really, really wide.

'My journalism is serious, Gareth. Don't be rude.' Alys sulked.

Gareth joined us at the table, sitting opposite me. My exits were narrowing.

'Conor-lad, get the kid a Coke.' He swigged from 'my' beer.

'Do you live here?' I said.

'We do now, little fella.' Gareth laughed, then said, 'Nah, we move around a lot. Got a camper van. Maybe that's why we weren't affected – too free-spirited for brain control.' His expression changed and he became serious. 'Tell me about this safe house.'

'I need to use the loo. Is that OK?' I needed to get away from these people. If I was lucky there might be a window I could escape through.

And what does he mean about 'brain control'?

'Sure,' Gareth said, smiling. He had a scraggy brown beard that moved in patches as he spoke. 'In a minute. Squeeze it in.'

He wasn't exactly stopping me from leaving but I knew that he would.

Conor handed me a Coca-Cola and I took two big swigs, despite genuinely needing the loo. It fizzed up my nose and I snorted. It didn't help my nerves.

'So, the safe house?' Gareth repeated.

'Gloria's dad is taking us somewhere safe; a place where kids can go to wait for their parents to get better. She said Conor should come.' I looked at my cousin and swallowed down a burp. 'But you don't have to. It's fine. I'll just let them know you're here when we get there, then Aunty Suzie can come get—'

Gareth slammed his meaty hand on the table, making my glass jump.

'You won't be telling anyone where we are. Conor, get the door.'

He meant 'lock us in', I knew it. I opened my mouth to speak but nothing came out. All I could think about was how Conor had left Jos, and now I had too. I wondered how long he and Gloria would play gigantic foam football before they realized I was in trouble. Would she come for me?

Conor went to the front door and locked it. I could see now that the smashed glass was from where they'd broken into the pub – a small pane by the top bolt was missing.

Alys gave me a friendly squeeze, in the most unfriendly way I'd ever experienced. 'Don't take it personally. We just want to keep our heads down until we've sussed a few things out. So you'll need to stay too. Don't worry, it'll be fun.'

Gareth added, 'Besides, you don't want to go trusting everyone you meet these days.'

15

ONE IN, ONE OUT

26 December

I tried to calm down by picturing my escape through an imagined tiny bathroom window – if my captors ever let me use the loo. I really did need to go, and I almost wet myself when Gareth suddenly leapt from his seat and thundered through the door behind the bar into what I assumed was the kitchen.

'Who wants an ice cream?'

Alys ran after him and Conor took the opportunity to turn to me and glare. 'Don't mess this up for me, man,' he said, quietly.

'I won't. You don't need me here. You don't want me here. Just let me go.' I glanced towards the kitchen.

'Yeah, OK.' Conor nodded for me to leave but then grabbed my arm. 'Look, I'm sorry, OK. It's not that I don't like you, or Jos. I do. But you want to go with Gloria and her dad and I prefer to stay with Alys and Gareth. We've both made our choice. What makes their place any better than hanging here?'

'You just want to drink beer.' I frowned.

I thought Conor would call me a baby or something like that but he didn't. He looked at me seriously. 'Just watch out for yourself in this *safe house*. Rounding people up "for their own safety" isn't always done with the best intentions and you can be too trusting at times. Do you even know where it is?'

A chill ran down my spine like a cold tap with a drip, but I didn't have a chance to shake it off, as just then there was a crash and a scream from the kitchen.

'Go!' insisted Conor, flapping his hand towards the door before running towards the commotion.

The kitchen door swung shut but not before I heard Conor shouting, 'Oh God! Oh no . . . NO!'

I hesitated. It was like the herd in the dune grass

all over again. I should go, get as far away as possible, get back to Jos, Gloria and Kika and leave.

'Help him!' Alys sounded hysterical.

I spun on my heels and ran to the kitchen door. I didn't need the loo any more.

'What happened?' I asked, trying to make sense of the scene. Alys's hands were in her hair, soil was scattered across the floor, and Gareth was curled in a ball on the floor, twitching in a spasm, moaning, shivering. I made a move towards him but Conor stopped me.

'Don't.' He pointed to what was clearly a newly dead mushroom-tree on the counter at the back of the room, shrivelled and grey and pulsing.

So it is *the plants.*

'But how? They can't get you once they're already dead . . . can they?'

Alys was rubbing Gareth's back vigorously. 'It wasn't dead.' Her voice was shrill with panic.

Then, the plant made an awful cracking, popping sound, and split open along its length, spewing black goo all over itself.

'I don't understand,' I said. This didn't fit with my theory about the cold killing them. The pub was warm. The open fire had probably been lit all Christmas Eve, so the pub hadn't got cold like the other houses in the village. Even though Gareth's fire-making skills were terrible, the pub was still warm so how . . .

Then I saw. Gareth had opened one of the giant chest freezers. The ones that let out a whoosh of frigid air when you open them.

'All this for a bloody ice cream,' Alys said, beginning to cry.

'The cold *did* kill it. I was right!' I covered my mouth to stop from breathing in any spores or pollen or toxic who-knows-what.

Gareth groaned again and staggered to his feet. Half crawling, stumbling, he crashed past us, sending a basket of cutlery and ketchup bottles flying, and banged into the front door, groping around for the handle with whatever was left of his human consciousness. He yanked it open with alarming force, and a little help from the wind, and then lurched into the street.

Alys ran after him yelling, 'Gareth! No, come back. Stay, you can get warm in here.' She turned to Conor and me. 'Help me get him back, we can get the fire lit proper.'

My heart tore in two at her desperate pleading, but I didn't think keeping him warm was the answer.

'No, Alys!' yelled Conor. 'We don't know if it's catching.'

Gareth stumbled again, pulling against Alys's grip on his leather jacket. His moans changed and became a growl and his eyes flashed with rage at her. The whites turned grey then black and as his skin paled, black veins crawled across his cheeks, forking like lightning. Spit flew from the corner of his mouth and he almost pulled Alys over. Conor tried to weigh in too, but Gareth was a big lad, and too strong. He jerked all over like something was possessing him, taking over his body, then he opened his mouth and roared in fury. Staring right at me, his irises morphed in a rush from hazel to bright crimson, the colour rippling with light. He arched his back, took in a deep but stuttering breath and then . . . he went limp. His arms dropped to his side like a doll's and his eyes were cast down. I could tell he was still pulling towards the beach but the fight in him was gone.

He was one of *them* now, heading south.

I wondered how I had gone from being so afraid of him in the pub, to this. I wondered if I told *him* now to drink a beer, he would.

Conor pulled me aside. 'Go back to Gloria. I'm going to stay here and try to help Alys get him somewhere safe.' He looked across at Alys, who was shaking and sobbing, trying to stop Gareth from heading to the sea. 'Then . . . I'll come and find you and Jos.' He ran to Alys and put his arm around her, shouting back to me, 'You stay safe, little cuz. And keep your eyes peeled for those weird Christmas trees. Remember, we don't know where they came from.'

I thought of a hundred reasons why I should stay and help too, but instead, I ran back towards the campsite, and my little brother.

16

THE FRIARY

26 December

Outside the campsite reception, with its beach balls and crabbing nets now shaking furiously in the wind, was a smart-looking BMW. The engine was running – I could just hear it over the wind and Gloria's yelling. She ran towards me holding her hood in place, a mixture of concern and relief on her face.

'Where is he?' She grabbed my sleeve and dragged me to the car. 'Get in.' I ignored her question and slid on to the back seat beside Jos.

'Mase! We thought we'd have to leave without you.' Jos pulled me into a hug. 'Where's Conor?'

'Had a bit of trouble,' I said, grimacing in that

funny way people do to suggest everything is OK really. 'What happened on the cliff?' I asked Gloria, changing the subject. Kika huffed from the floor as my foot nudged her. 'Did the rope work?'

Gloria's dad twisted himself around in the driver's seat. I winced, expecting to be told off, but he had a kind look on his face. 'That's very thoughtful of you, Masen. I'm sorry to say we lost a few people. But Lily and her boys acted quickly and they were able to encourage the Infected away from the edge. They're quite compliant once they get going in the right direction, and they're all heading to the beach now, like the others. It's not ideal, but they'll be safe. We've managed to get barriers up on the beach too, so the tide can't sweep them away, and we have people there to watch them, give them blankets, make sure no one else gets hurt. Mostly, the Infected already there are exhausted, sitting down, calm, waiting for rescue.' He looked pretty exhausted himself.

'Oh, that's good. I mean – better than I thought it would be.' The thought of the infected people just sitting on the beach all night in the cold and dark made me shiver, but it was better than the alternative.

'Dad and everyone at the Friary – that's where we're going – just want to help people,' said Gloria, clicking in her seatbelt. 'And more help will be on its way soon.'

Gloria's dad reached out his hand. 'I'm Dr Owain Haradwaith, by the way. Dr H is fine – I know it's a bit of a mouthful. Pleased to meet you, despite the circumstances.'

I shook his hand and as Gloria slammed her door closed, Conor's words about 'being too trusting' popped into my head. But I was too tired and overwhelmed to worry about it. I was just happy to be back with Jos.

'Masen Williams. Mase is fine. And this is Jos.'

'Can we go to the cottage and get our things?' said Jos.

'Straight to the Fri for you,' said Dr H, as the windscreen wipers jumped into life. 'Just to be on the safe side. It's my family home, rather grand I'm embarrassed to say, but it makes a great temporary shelter for all the local kids. This thing seems to only affect adults. I'm not sure why but . . . did Gloria mention that as well as being a doctor, I'm a botanist – a plant scientist? I'm doing a little research into what might have happened.' He turned to face the front. 'Anyway, don't you worry. The emergency services are on their way – helicopters and ambulances – to help the adults. We're working with them, and they know all about the Fri. They'll be making sure everyone finds their loved ones as soon as possible.'

And with that, we pulled out and away from the campsite and towards our next port of call.

I wanted to keep track of where we were going, but by the time we drove through the gates of the Friary I realized I'd spent the entire journey staring out of the window into nothing but my own thoughts.

The Friary was at the end of a short road of elm trees: a huge red-brick building that looked a lot like it was being eaten alive by ivy. We crunched across the wide gravel drive, bordered by towering bushes that shook in what had now become a wintry gale. Dr H parked beside a minivan and honked the horn.

The front door opened, and a man in overalls ushered us inside, out of the sideways sleet. 'Welcome, my beauties,' he said with a warm smile.

'I'm Dafydd – cleaner, groundskeeper, caretaker, general dogsbody.' He said his name with a 'th' sound at the end, with the same Welsh accent that Dr H and Alys had. He was much younger than Dr H, with a short beard and friendly eyes. 'Welcome, welcome. The others are waiting in the hallway. Come on out of the storm.'

My stomach clenched at the prospect of meeting a bunch of new people who probably all knew one another and didn't need any more friends. Before we'd left for Wales, Mum had said that Jos and I could go into the village with Conor and maybe meet some local kids while we were on holiday. How ironic that we were sort of doing exactly that.

As we walked into the toasty hallway of the Friary my brain filled up with too much information. People, noise, colour. Every surface was decorated for a homely Christmas. Candles smelling of Christmas puddings and cinnamon warmed the air. The portraits and framed certificates were hung with holly and ivy and a huge Christmas tree rose up beside a central staircase. It must've needed a crane to get it in there. Even I gasped at the sight of it.

I'd almost forgotten, but it was still Boxing Day – past dinner time if my stomach rumbles were anything to go by. By now, we should have been watching *The Gruffalo's Child* for the millionth time while eating alternate handfuls of chocolate and cheese. I should be buried in a brand-new graphic novel and Jos should be building something epic in Lego. I wouldn't even mind listening to Conor's rubbish music if it meant having Christmas back.

Dafydd grabbed an iPad from a small table by the front door. Only then did I register that the lights were on! And that Dafydd had unplugged the iPad from a charger. How did this place have power? Or did that mean the power was back on everywhere? I wanted to ask but Dafydd was herding us towards the other kids. *Wait, what about* . . . I looked back towards the front door. 'Kika?' I asked.

'We've got a couple of kids who are scared of dogs,' said Dafydd. 'So Dr H will take her to the stables.'

At my worried expression, Dr H added, 'It's warm and full of hay and toys and she'll be well looked after by Lily and Dafydd. You can check on her any time and take her for walks, if this storm ever lets up.'

I nodded, too tired to argue even if I'd wanted to. And I didn't want to – it wasn't my style.

Dafydd tapped the iPad and passed it to me. 'Pop your details on there, matey.' Then, he turned to address everyone. 'I'm sorry for all your troubles – I'm sure you're worried about your missing families, but I for one am glad you've found your way here to us at the Fri. We are going to look after you all good and proper.' He looked anxious as he spoke and I wondered if he was missing family or friends too.

The tablet displayed a spreadsheet with kids' names, parents' names and home addresses. I made a quick estimate that there were about thirty kids' names on the list, then filled in our details at the bottom. I couldn't help thinking about Conor. Even though he'd left Jos alone, I was worried about him.

I pushed aside my complicated thoughts about my cousin and almost typed in Kika's name after mine. It felt silly, but also like we were losing too many parts of ourselves. First our entire family, then Conor, and now Kika – even if she was just in another part of the grounds. We were supposed to stay together, but now there were only two of us left. I put my arm around Jos and pulled him tight to me. Nothing was going to split us up.

17

IT *IS* ICE CREAM DAY

26 December

Dafydd took back the iPad, called out our names and had us stand in family groups. Then he handed a key to me, and to the eldest in each of the other groups. Three kids were singles and they got to share. 'Now, can you all tell the time?'

There was a skitter of nervous nods and kids said, 'yes' and 'of course' and everyone looked relieved at being asked such a simple, ordinary question. One with a simple, ordinary answer.

'Good,' said Dafydd. 'There's some stuff to tell you about, like where to get dinner and best spots for footie and which days are ice cream days, but first I want you to go to your new rooms and flop on the beds. No bouncing mind, just flopping. Lie down, breathe, just be. Now, where's my dream team . . .' He held his hands out to the single kids. 'Tell each other your names and say "hi". Then, at six thirty, all you have to do is stand outside your bedroom doors. Gloria or I will collect you and take you to the hall for some supper, perhaps a nice cup of tea and some jammy scones too. What say you?' He nodded a sort of full stop to his speech.

Everyone mumbled 'OK' and Dafydd clapped his hands together. 'Right then, my beauties. Follow me.'

Jos pulled me close. 'I haven't got my toothbrush,' he whispered.

I laughed to show him that it didn't matter one little bit. 'Me neither.'

Dafydd led us up the wide carpeted flight of stairs that encircled the enormous tree. Lights twinkled and glass baubles shone. I saw Jos's face reflected in one and he was smiling. We followed the crowd along a corridor with rooms off on either side.

'Used to be a hotel, in case you're wondering,' said Dafydd. 'And we have our own generator – hence the power being on.'

The group of three found their room and giggled gleefully. At first, their happy reaction surprised me, but then even I got a little excited, spotting the door number that matched our key and discovering our new room. I wasn't ready to think everything would be OK, it was too soon for that, but it definitely could've been worse. Our room was huge! It had two big beds, with deep, fluffy duvets and pillows like small hills.

I turned to thank Gloria, but she was busy helping other kids. It felt weird – as though she wasn't ours any more – and I realized two things: one, she was part of the team at the Friary, not just tagging along with her dad; and two, I had come to rely on her, maybe even think of her as a friend, even in the short time since we'd met.

Jos and I did as we'd been told and flopped with an exhale, one on each massive bed.

'You OK, Jos?'

'Not too bad.' Jos's voice was muffled by the pillow that seemed to have eaten him. He peered over the edge. 'I hope it's an ice cream day today.'

I checked the little bedside clock. 'Only half an hour until we find out,' I said, with as much enthusiasm and normality as I could manage. Exhaustion had hit me like a solid wall.

'Do you think Conor will be OK? And Kika?' said Jos. 'And Mum and Dad and Nanny . . .'

I zoned out before he got to the end of the family roll call. I had to keep going for Jos, but I was low on energy, and his questions were wearing me out. I needed my quiet time more than ice cream.

'They'll be fine,' I said, grateful Jos hadn't seen the people on the cliff. 'Conor was with a girl called Alys. She was . . . nice.' I hated lying to him, but I was running on empty. 'And remember what Gloria said – there's a treatment and our family are probably in hospital already.' I tried to smile but I knew it looked fake. 'Jos, why don't you have a poke around the room, check out the cupboards. I just need to shut my eyes for a sec.'

'You need some space, Mase?' He snorted. 'Space-Mase! Space-Mase on the space race,' he sang, jumping off the bed and throwing open the wardrobe. 'Ooh, there's clothes! And boxes of shoes and a load of hats and—'

'Shh.' I immediately felt bad, but I couldn't bear it any more. I needed to recharge.

'Sorry, Mase.'

I barely heard him as my brain went numb.

The next thing I knew, someone was banging on the door and Jos was shaking me awake, his face bobbing in and out of view. I sat up and Jos went to the door.

'He fell asleep!' I heard him say.

'That's OK, he deserves it.'

I tried to place the voice – it wasn't Mum or Suzie, or . . . it all returned like a gale slamming a door.

Gloria. The Friary.

I rolled off the bed, stiff and aching. My head had more stuffing in it than the duvet and my legs didn't want to move. I looked at the clock – it was six forty.

'Sorry,' I said. Sort of to Gloria, sort of to everyone else in the corridor. *Ah!* Was I the only one who'd fallen asleep? *What a plank.*

'No need for apologies,' said Dafydd from the end of the corridor. 'I like an afternoon nap myself. But now we're all here – onwards!' He boomed out this last and it cut through the dense fog in my brain.

'Dafydd?' a small girl close to the groundskeeper piped up. 'How long do we have to stay here? I want my mum.'

'I know, poppet. I'm sorry she's not here right now, but you've asked a very good question, although it's not one I can answer for sure.'

I could tell he wasn't the type to sugar-coat the truth, even for kids. I was both alarmed and comforted by that at the same time.

Dafydd took a deep breath. 'So maybe you know that a lot of adults have got an illness. There's a cure, we know that, so you don't need to worry, but what with the storm blocking the roads and it being Christmas week and all, getting help where it's needed is taking longer than usual. The reason we took all your names and addresses is so that we can find your parents. Then, if they're well, you can leave. The more healthy adults we find, the more people there are to help us look. So, it could be a while before you get to leave, or it could be tomorrow.'

'Or today?' said a short kid in the middle of the group.

'Right. But you wouldn't want to leave today,

not on an ice cream day.' Dafydd looked deadly serious.

A giggle rippled through the small kids. 'It *is* ice cream day!' one of them cheered.

18

SILENT NIGHT

26–27 December

We followed Dafydd down the stairs and this time, instead of the tree, I looked at the paintings on the wall. Plants. All of them.

'You like plants?' asked Dafydd.

'I like art,' I replied.

'Ah, me too. I paint a lot, actually. Nature, like these. What art do you like?'

'Anime mostly, but these are really good.' A painting labelled *Serenity One* caught my eye. It was so detailed, like it was painted from life, but it couldn't have been. It was too weird, with too many colours and textures: the huge, bright flowers were beautiful, but there were also soft, velvety fungi wrapped around them, almost like they were locked in battle. It was a bit unsettling and I stared at it for so long that Dafydd began to frown at me.

'Now that everyone's here,' he said, 'the front door and main gate will be locked for safety. So, all you need to worry about is that door . . .' He pointed both hands in front like a crew member on a plane doing the safety announcement. 'That takes you to the dining room slash games room, and beyond to the kitchen, then outside to the back garden, the allotments, the lawn, the orchard, the old monastery ruins and the tennis courts. Oh, and the pool.'

Another collective gasp.

'There's a pool?' cried Jos.

Dafydd grinned, pleased with himself. 'Yes, my lovelies, there's a pool. A heated pool at that. You can all have a splash about after something to eat. There's spare kit you can use.'

Dafydd looked back at the painting, then led us into the dining hall. It was full of yet more kids – too many to count – sitting on benches at a long, grand table, tucking eagerly into what looked like chicken soup. I perched on the end of a table, with

Jos opposite.

The kid next to me extended a hand, as a strong gust of wind rattled the windows. 'This storm is intense, right? Hi, I'm Tam. They/them, but I don't mind if you forget sometimes. You're new, right? Don't worry, I've been here since day one; yeah, I know that was only yesterday but a lot's happened, right? Happy Christmas!' They took a slurp of soup. 'You should eat. I helped set everything up here, if you're interested, and I know everything you need to know . . . maybe more than you want to know.' Tam stared at me intently as if they were looking for something behind my eyes. I covered my awkwardness by eating the delicious and very appreciated soup. Tam carried on talking. 'Mostly, you get to do what you want, which is cool, but if you're sad, you can talk to anyone if you need to. She's nice.' Tam pointed to the person making a beeline for us with a pot of tea, a tray of scones and a calm, welcoming smile. 'That's Lily. She's here with her kids. They're older than us and they help out here too. And at the beach. They usually head there after breakfast.'

Gloria and Dr H had mentioned Lily a few times

so it was nice to properly meet her. She radiated calm and I could feel it having an effect on me. It was so welcome.

'Hi Tam, hi you two. I'm Lily: cook, electrician, physiotherapist, top goalscorer in football and a survivor. Shout if you need anything. Unless you want to know which goes on first.' She pointed to the scones. 'Jam or cream first? I can't pick sides over that one, there'd be an uproar,' she said with a wink. Then she left us.

'Jam first, obvs,' said Tam, pushing their scraped-clean bowl aside and grabbing a scone from the pile.

I hadn't known it was up for debate, but I copied them, and Jos copied me.

'Do you know what's going on, Tam? Does anyone know? I wanted to ask Dr H but I've not seen him since . . .'

He took Kika.

'Dr H is busy. A lot.' So far, Tam had talked as though it was the last day on Earth and they had to say everything all at once, but when they said that, they spoke slowly, meaningfully. 'He's trying to save the infected people. Gloria said it's something to do with mushrooms, some kind of fungus pandemic that only affects adults. She said it can be treated with really basic medicine, but getting it to them was difficult.'

Because they're all at the bottom of a cliff.

The thought washed over me before I could stop it. It was followed by more unwanted thoughts: people in ditches, in rivers, in the sea.

I don't know how long I was sat there, not responding, but Tam nudged me. I must've zoned out again.

'I said, did you open yours? Presents, I mean. I burnt through all mine before I even noticed me ma hadn't come home. Feel right great about that I can tell you.' For a moment Tam seemed to have run out of things to say, but . . . no, they were just stopping for air. 'It's about the cruellest thing I can imagine – Christmas being gone like that. Nice one, universe. Way to go. I haven't exactly had the best year. Me and Ma were fighting a lot; she calls me Wild Thing, like from that book where the plants cover everything in the little boy's bedroom and . . . she wasn't even home on Christmas Eve, so the last time I saw her she was working and too busy to even . . .' Tam scraped their chair back and stood up, the look of a wild creature in their eyes.

Lily walked quickly over. 'Tam, can you give me a hand with the ice creams?' There was something in Lily's expression I couldn't place – a need to calm Tam down or stop them from saying any more.

Tam bit their lip and followed Lily towards the kitchen.

Jos and I finished our tea, then took supermarket-brand Fabs from the ice cream trolley. Then, Dafydd announced that we were free to use the swimming pool until bedtime at nine, and that there were a variety of sizes of clean swimsuits in a box in the pool changing rooms. If we didn't want to swim, we could take turns – thirty minutes each – on the PlayStations in the games room or watch a DVD.

Everything we could want or need was at our disposal.

But I just wanted to go home.

I lay under the warm duvet listening to Jos's gentle breathing as he slept. It felt like I'd been trying to sleep for ages, like time had been stretched. Yesterday seemed like a lifetime ago. How could all of this have happened so quickly?

I ran my hand over the sheets, smooth, fresh, unfamiliar. I'd told Jos to pretend we were on holiday in a fancy hotel – made up a whole scenario where we were mega-rich and travelling the world. We pretended to make a TikTok about our travels and Jos giggled his way through telling his 'followers' that we'd been to Disneyland – the most exotic place he could think of. *Pretended*, because our phones were now out of battery. We weren't allowed to charge them, despite the generator that powered the Friary. Tam had asked Dafydd and been told they were non-essential.

The make-believe had worked for Jos . . . and probably the bedtime hot chocolate had helped too. I couldn't face it though, and now I was wide awake and alert. I saw shadows in every corner, startled every time the curtains twitched in the breeze, and listened for the occasional padding of footsteps on the hallway carpet.

And that was just the things that were real. When I closed my eyes I saw black veins on pale grey skin, Conor falling into never-ending razor-sharp grass, Gareth jerking as he turned. And in the background, the sound of the Infected moaning like the wind. I tried to recentre myself, I breathed slowly, counted to ten, held Mum's compass against my cheek, but it wasn't enough.

As quietly as I could, to not wake Jos, I slipped out of bed and crept to the window, intending to open it a little wider to let some of the hot stuffy air out and some cool fresh air slap the nightmares away.

But as my hand touched the window handle, I paused.

I blinked twice in case this was more shenanigans from my imagination, but nope – someone really was outside on the lawn.

The bedside clock showed 2 a.m. Odd time for a stroll, and not exactly a nice night for it, but maybe they couldn't sleep either.

I hesitated, not wanting to open the window further in case the mystery nightwalker saw me and thought I was spying on them. I slunk into the shadows. And spied on them.

I couldn't make out any features, just the shape of a person. They were crouched by the boundary hedge, concealed in darkness. Then they stood, paused, walked to the right and then . . . disappeared.

I rubbed my eyes to be sure, but I wasn't seeing things. They'd vanished. There must be a gap in the hedge . . . but was the person out there infected, or not? I tried to tell myself it was probably one of Lily's older sons, who I'd not met yet, but all I could think was that the Infected were here too, in the garden, surrounding us . . .

Stop it!

I pulled the curtains closed again and gripped them in my fist.

No. Something about the way they'd stood up and walked – crept – about made me certain it was someone uninfected. And while it was one thing to worry about Jos or Conor, I couldn't worry about a complete stranger . . . I needed to keep the space in my brain for things that would help keep me and Jossy safe.

I crept back into bed, keeping my eye on Jos, making sure not to wake him. I lay there, still and stiff in the dark, thinking, not thinking, worrying, not worrying.

Stop it, stop it, stop . . .

19

GONE

27 December

'Morning, Joss-man!' My enthusiasm sounded way too fake to me, but Jossy didn't seem to notice. 'Sleep well?'

He nodded, rolled over and jumped out of bed. I had barely slept after spying the strange wanderer during the night, so I didn't have the energy to leap up like him.

'I dreamt I was a doctor, making everyone better. And Gloria was a vet and she found Fran and made her all better.'

'That sounds like a good dream.' I slunk out of bed, trudged sleepily to the window and threw open the curtains. Rain pelted the deserted lawn, lashing about in the wind, and I wondered if I'd been dreaming too.

'Do you think breakfast will be ready yet?' Jos was already getting dressed.

'Go wash your face, then we'll go find out, yeah?'

Jos went to go but I lunged for him, grabbing him by the hoody and pulling him into me. I couldn't help it – I was supposed to be taking care of his needs, but *I* needed a hug.

'Love you, Mase,' he said, half buried in my armpit. I held him there longer than was probably normal, but it felt good.

Once we were both dressed, we headed out. Gloria was on the stairs holding hands with two young girls.

'Morning, you two!' she sang out. 'Lovely weather, hey?' Her grimace told me she was joking.

'Did anyone leave last night?' I blurted out.

Gloria looked quizzically at me. 'Leave? You mean, get sent home? No, you're a bit hopeful, aren't you? Actually, one person left on Christmas night – turned out their parents weren't infected after all. But no one since then. Why do you ask?'

I brushed it off with a wave of my hand.

'Nothing. It's nothing. I think I was dreaming.' I chuckled in the way Aunty Suzie does . . . did . . . when she wanted to change the subject from something awkward.

Gloria squeezed the little ones' hands. 'Come on then, let's get breakfast.'

I took Jos's hand and followed the smell of warm pastries. Halfway down the stairs, I paused. The *Serenity One* painting was gone, replaced by an ordinary-looking photo of a beach.

Somehow, breakfast was jolly . . . rowdy even, almost as though this entire horrible thing wasn't happening and we were all on some kind of group residential. I tried to let all the noise and cheer in, but I couldn't. I just felt lost.

It wasn't all bad, though. Jos seemed OK and he was fitting in with the crowd much better than me. Dad sometimes called me *resilient*, but perhaps that description fit Jos better.

I sat beside a lad my age, who was hitting an old-fashioned radio with the heel of his hand. 'It's broken,' he said and dropped the radio to the table. 'There was a message coming from it yesterday,' he explained. 'Something about staying indoors, not following the Infected. It was a police message.'

'It's probably run out of battery,' yelled someone from far down the table. 'There'll be no news yet. Anyway, what we need is mobile signal so we can get on the internet . . . Hey, Mase!'

Jos nudged me. The someone shouting was Tam and they were waving furiously at me, seemingly unaware that they were yelling over the top of everyone else. 'Come and sit with us. We'll make space. There's loads of room.'

There wasn't, but Tam flapped their hands at the people sitting nearby and everyone shuffled up, leaving two empty seats, one beside them and one opposite. It felt super awkward, but after that, Jos and I kind of had to go and sit there. I avoided making eye contact as much as possible as I walked up the entire length of the table, but soon realized that no one was staring at me. They were all goggle-eyed at the food Lily and her two sons were laying out. I tried to study the almost grown-up lads as they served breakfast but I couldn't tell if any of them were my mystery person. One of them caught me staring and gave me an odd, thin smile. They seemed tired, but then, wasn't everyone?

'There are chickens beside the allotments, so there are always eggs,' explained Tam. 'Go on, have a boiled egg, they're just right – runny and perfect for dipping.' Beside the eggs was a pile of toast.

There was also a Jenga-like heap of croissants and pains au chocolat, jugs of squash, and lashings of butter and jam. But faced with what was undeniably a delicious breakfast, my stomach rolled.

How can anyone eat at a time like this?

Tam was going on about there also being cereal but that the milk was gross, but all I could think about was them saying there was 'no news'. It was so final, like once the news stopped happening, life stopped happening.

I scanned the room for Dr H or Gloria, desperate to ask at least some of the hundred questions I had. I should've asked Lily as she was setting the table . . .

But you were too busy being weird.

I leant closer to Tam. 'Isn't there any way to find out what's happening out there?' We'd had no contact with the outside world since the storm.

Tam gave me their intense stare. 'Nope. Still no

internet. The mobile phone masts got blown over in the storm, and this old place hasn't got any sort of cable or satellite. It's the butt end of nowhere.' They giggled. 'I'm going for a walk in a minute to try and get a signal.'

'Don't go out there,' said an older kid. 'You'll get zombified.'

I winced. 'It's not anything "out there" – it's those little Christmas trees with the mushrooms on. You know the ones I mean? When they die they . . .' Gareth's face flashed before me. 'I've seen it.'

Another kid scoffed. 'Nah, it's another pandemic. You catch it like a cold and it makes you vanish. My Gran had a cough, then *poof*, disappeared.'

'Don't be daft!' said another. 'It's nothing like a cold. You wouldn't say that if you'd seen one of them. I saw two—'

'And I saw loads—' said another.

'It's not natural, that's for sure,' Tam interrupted before it turned into a competition. 'It was probably made in a lab, like an experiment gone wrong. What do you think about that, *Mase*?'

I didn't know what to think and Tam was examining me again, eyes burning into me. My skin felt tight. They leant close to me.

'Can I trust you?' they whispered.

A quick glance along the table showed me everyone else had gone back to their breakfast, too hungry to talk, Jos included. I nodded.

'What would you say if I told you that I don't think this "safe house" is safe at all? That we're being watched.'

A sharp pain pulsed in the side of my head, and I rubbed at my temple. Lily, who'd returned from the kitchen with more toast, caught my eye, then Tam's.

'Oh, hey, are you all right?' asked Tam, suddenly light and breezy again. 'Sorry – have I been going on? I know I talk too much. It's nerves. Mum says I have to make noise when it's silent 'cause it makes me anxious. And now I'm making you anxious.' Tam took a breath. 'Sorry.' They waved Lily over. 'Lil, Masen's got a headache. Can he have a painkiller?'

'Or just a cup of tea?' I ventured.

'Of course, lovey, you can have both. Although there's only powdered milk – not enough power to run the big fridge.' She smiled an apology.

'That's fine, thanks.'

'But if it's a headache you should eat something. You've been through a rough experience, and I'll bet you've not eaten properly.'

I thought of Fran stealing the cold meat and Suzie and Benedict going crazy about it, and a sob got lodged in my throat. I forced it down along with a bite of croissant, but then I couldn't help wondering if I'd ever see Nanny Sasha again or receive another hand-drawn piece of gift-wrapping from Mum and I cough-sobbed it all out on to the table.

A boy beside me shouted 'EWWW!' at the top of his voice, but I didn't care. I shoved back my chair, tugged off my glasses and ran, crying out of the door towards . . . I didn't know where I was going, I just needed to be gone.

20

IT'S OK TO NOT BE FINE

27 December

Sometimes, when I'm anxious, my brain hides in a safe place. It still works but part of it sort of powers down. Basically, I zone out. This time, when my brain switched back on again, Gloria, Jos and Tam were sitting beside me on a haybale in the barn. None of them said anything, but Tam handed me a mug of hot tea and Gloria put a hand on my shoulder. Kika was licking my ankle.

I sipped the tea, which soothed my poor, panicked brain. 'Thanks,' I said, embarrassed now at having made such a scene.

Lily arrived, headache tablet in hand, and she passed it to me along with a glass of water, then scratched Kika behind the ears. 'Take your time, Masen. Can I get you anything else?'

I wondered what Conor would say to me right now. Maybe: *Pull your socks up*, which made me chuckle. How had things got so bad that I even missed Conor?

'No, thank you. I'm fine.'

'It's OK to not be fine,' said Lily. 'And you don't need to worry about Jos either – we'll take care of you both.'

My shoulders relaxed. I didn't want to admit out loud what a relief that was.

'Yeah,' said Tam. 'I know what it's like – this whole situation is so scary. I deal with it by getting curious, asking too many questions. It's fear of the unknown, right? So I want to know everything – knowledge is power, right? What about you, Mase?'

Lily shot Tam a look as if to say 'leave Mase alone', which I was grateful for. There was something about Tam I liked, they were so friendly and open, but the conspiracy theories hurt my head.

'Hey, the rain's stopped,' said Gloria, and I silently thanked her for changing the subject. 'Do you fancy a walk around the gardens with me, Mase? It might help your head. Poor Kika's not getting enough walks with this weather.'

I nodded. A walk sounded great and now that my brain was functioning properly again, I thought it would be the perfect opportunity to reconnect with Gloria and ask her a few questions.

Jos stayed back with Tam, while Gloria and I set out, squelching across the soaking grass. She hadn't seen her dad to ask about the rescue efforts, so I switched to my other planned conversation: the mystery hedge and the disappearing person in the middle of the night. I led Kika closer to it to see if she could smell anything interesting.

'Oh!' I was surprised at how glad I was to see footprints in the sodden ground: proof that I hadn't imagined it – someone *had* been there! Kika sniffed the prints and barked once, loudly.

'Look at that,' I said, reaching out to touch the hedge. It was actually two hedges, one that went just behind the other. From the front, it looked like all one hedge.

'Clever.' I stepped into the gap and 'disappeared'

like the person I'd seen in the night. Gloria followed, looking as puzzled as I felt.

The footprints continued along a narrow path that led through an overgrown area, thick with brambles, nettles and poisonous lords-and-ladies berries, eventually reaching a door in the ground that looked like the entrance to an underground bunker, or cellar. To the right was a black box with a blank screen, on a pole.

'Palm entry, maybe. Or facial recognition?' I looked into the screen and pulled a face while Gloria tugged at the door handle.

Gloria looked worried. 'I wonder what's down there. Maybe your mystery person.'

'Or a secret stash of fresh milk,' I said. 'Just don't tell Tam.'

Gloria put an ear to the door. 'I can't hear anything. Maybe they're hoarding gallons of it. And cheese.'

'What? There's no cheese either?' I forced out a smile.

'It's probably boring stuff, like generator fuel or lawnmowers or something,' said Gloria. Either way, it was a dead end, both to the overgrown path and also to the mystery of my disappearing stranger.

Then something struck me. 'How come you didn't know this was here? Don't you live here?'

Gloria's face tightened. 'Not really. I live with my mum. I was just here for the holidays.'

I got the feeling I'd put my foot in it, so I shut up. So much for Tam's idea that knowledge is power – I quite often got in trouble for asking too many questions. Or the wrong questions.

We walked back to the lawn and were greeted by the sound of giggling. A group of kids were running across the grass in dressing gowns and trainers, sockless and clutching towels. They raced from the swimming pool building back to the main house as if they might freeze if they went any slower. The youngest resident, Will, called to Gloria, waving enthusiastically.

To the right of the main house, Dafydd was emerging from the allotment with a wheelbarrow. It was piled high with bags of compost and something that looked like a suitcase underneath. He flashed us a broad grin and I smiled back.

From the corner of my eye, I saw Jossy waving at me from behind a downstairs window. It felt weird and for a moment I couldn't work out why, and then it hit me . . .

Everyone was happy.

How was it possible, with everything that was happening? In fact, how had this happened to us at all? It was too big, too unnatural, too unlikely.

But it had, just like so many calamities before. The Black Death, the Great Influenza epidemic, Covid-19. Why did we still think it wouldn't happen to us?

'Mase?' Gloria ducked her face close to mine and her concerned expression snapped me out of my daydream.

'Sorry, I was miles away. Just thinking—'

She grabbed my hand, stopping me mid-sentence. 'Don't. It does no good. Come on, how about a bite to eat now?'

Lily was right. After tucking into an ample lunch, I felt better. I also found an awesome chess partner called Avi, and had some screen time with Jos. He wanted to play *Overwatch*, which he knows he's not allowed at home, so I chose something more calming. And after thirty minutes of *Animal Crossing* and a dinner I was surprisingly hungry for, we all gathered to watch a David Attenborough DVD that Dr H had put on.

Tam called us over and we sat with them on the carpet.

'According to Dr H, this DVD "explains a lot" about what's happened to the adults.' They did finger quotes in the air.

The calming voice on the TV narrated as an ant got infected by a fungus, and then marched to the top of a very tall blade of grass.

'What does it mean?' I asked, confused.

'This is what they've got, according to Dr H. A fungal infection that controls the mind. It's made all the adults walk in a southerly direction – for warmth, he said. Just like the fungus in the ant has made it climb to the top of that grass to find a high point.'

A kid in front of us turned and shushed Tam.

I swallowed; my mind was racing, thinking. *What was it Gloria said? Thinking does no good?* I leant closer. 'But why does the fungus want the ant to be so high up?'

In answer, the ant's head suddenly split open, and

sped-up footage showed a mushroom bursting out of it. Then the mushroom opened up like a flower and exploded spores into the air, spreading them far and wide.

And just like that, everything was awful again.

Panic erupted in the room. Some of the kids started crying, including Jos. I felt like throwing up. Some 'helpful' kid had paused the DVD so we didn't have to see any more, but it had stopped on a close-up of the poor brain-dead ant. Its eyes were fogged over, its antennae hanging limp.

Lily rushed in, not running, she never actually ran; instead, she strode calmly and purposefully . . . just really fast. She switched off the screen and urged us all to listen.

Apart from the occasional sniffle, the room was quiet.

'Everyone, I'd like you all to move into the dining area, as we have some good news . . . and a treat.'

That was enough to shift the mood and although we were all a bit shocked by what we'd seen, we all stood and slowly made our way to the benches.

Tam being Tam, however, needed to know more. 'The thing with the ant, though—'

Lily quickly shut Tam down. 'People are not ants, Tam. I'm sorry that took you all by surprise but don't worry, no one's head is exploding. Unless it's at the thought of a hot chocolate?'

21

LEAVING PARTY

27–28 December

Exploding heads were immediately forgotten. Laid out on the table for each of us was a paper cup of hot chocolate and a mince pie. Once again, I'd forgotten it was still the Christmas holiday. I bit into the sugary pastry and my senses were overwhelmed. In a good way this time. I glanced over at Jossy and saw he felt the same. People weren't ants, it was still the day after Boxing Day, the thing that had infected everyone was a fungus, and there was medicine. I squeezed Jossy's hand. Perhaps everything *would* be OK.

Dr H joined us, the iPad in his hand. 'I think Lily informed you that there was good news.

And indeed there is.' He sat down and sipped his own hot chocolate from a 'Ho-Ho-Ho' mug. 'Yasmin, Keren and Avi . . . would you stand up please?'

Two kids I'd seen earlier during the chilly swimming pool dash stood, slowly. Avi did the same.

'No need to look so worried. Quite the opposite, in fact. Your parents are safe and well and being looked after in Morriston Hospital in Swansea. Dafydd is ready with the car to take you to them.'

The three kids gasped, along with almost everyone else. I should've too, but instead, a wave of selfish disappointment swept over me. I wished it were me and Jos. Also, Avi was fifteen games to thirteen up against me in chess and I'd just sussed out one of his major tells – he always looked three steps ahead.

I was horrified at myself for being such a terrible friend and gave him a big thumbs up to make up for it. I'd have to give him my phone number before he left.

I wasn't the only one who reacted oddly to the others' good fortune. Tam was slumped in their chair, forehead creased and sighing in that way people do when they want you to ask what they're sighing about.

So I did.

But Dr H was watching us.

'Ask me later,' they said.

Dr H turned to address the audience. 'This will happen for all of you – and soon, I'm sure. It's a good sign that we're only three days in and already people are moving on.' He ushered Yasmin, Keren and Avi out of the door. I stood to wave to my chess partner, but he was gone.

'Now,' began Lily, 'it's late and I'm guessing you're all tired after a busy day. Let's get you all off to bed.'

At the sound of the word 'bed' I yawned, setting off a ripple around the room. Lily was right, we were all shattered.

I was practically asleep by the time my head hit the pillow.

I woke the next day, groggy from finally getting a proper sleep, but keen to find someone new to play chess with. I thought about asking Tam, but they were unusually quiet for the whole of breakfast. I meant to ask if they were OK, if they were missing family or one of the kids, but also, to be blunt, it was nice to have a rest from their constant chatting.

I made a mental note to ask later, but when later came, a girl called Ettie asked me to play chess, and Tam was in a private huddle with Gloria. They were both frowning at Tam's phone, their serious expressions offset by its fluffy purple case with charms hanging from it. Tam was the last of us to still have battery left. I almost interrupted them but the usual awkwardness took over. What if they didn't want me to disturb them? If they were having a private conversation and I barged in, they might feel like they had to invite me to join them and I might have interrupted at a crucial moment, and then they'd hate me for ever and shut me out of future conversa—

I overthought the whole thing to such an extent that Tam and Gloria finished whatever it was they were discussing and left the room, arms linked like besties.

I went for a wander instead. Jos was busy playing King of Tokyo and singing rude words to Christmas carols with some of the younger ones, so I took

Kika out for a nice long walk. It did the trick – the wind was still howling and it blew through me, clearing the cobwebs. I got lost in myself clambering over the old friary ruins, imagining the solemn monks that might have lived there, praying, gardening, kicking some Viking – or should it be Tudor? – butts. Having some time alone was a relief, and I felt centred again – enough to head back and find out what Tam was worried about.

Except I never got the chance, because when I got back to the house, Tam was gone.

As I went in the back door, Dafydd hurried me into the dining hall for lunch. He looked flustered, like I was late or something, and when I got there everyone was waiting. Dr H was at the head of the table, tearing into a bread roll, seeming close to bursting with energy. He looked like a kid with a secret he's absolutely, one hundred per cent going to tell you any minute.

He took a sip of black tea and then tapped a butter knife against his cup.

'Friends, if I could have your attention for just a moment. I have some wonderful news. You may have noticed that we are one short for lunch this afternoon. It is my pleasure to announce that Tam Playton was reunited with their family just after breakfast.'

Looks of confusion circled the table.

'I know . . . it's not how we usually do it.' He pressed a solemn hand to his heart. 'We had to rush them off, as the family couldn't wait. Sadly, Tam's grandmother is quite ill and their parents, who are remarkably well recovered, wanted Tam to see her before . . . well, you understand.'

A young girl put her hand up. 'Did Tam's nana have the fungus? Can you die of it then?'

Dr H held his hands out, palms down in a calming action. 'No, poppet. Nothing like that. She's ninety-eight. It's just her time. Hopefully, she'll be able to see her grandchild before the end.' He pushed back his chair and stood. 'Well, that's all from me. I'm needed elsewhere. Tuck in, my beauties. Your turn soon!' He picked up his mug and gave us all a kind smile before leaving us.

Gloria perched on the bench beside me. 'Hey, Masen, don't look so down,' she said.

I smiled. 'Sorry. I'm happy for them, I just

wanted to swap numbers. I know they talked A LOT, but I really liked them. They made the place . . . brighter, don't you think?'

Gloria nodded. 'Yup. I'll miss them too – they were like the OG, right? They were literally the first kid we collected. They basically helped us set up this place – helped make all the beds, got the food cupboards stocked . . . I'm glad Dad's doing what's best for them. And now Tam can help others, too. Isn't that what we all want? For the greater good.'

I wasn't sure what she meant by that at first, but then I realized that being here was like being on pause. Like we were waiting for something to do, some way to be useful, to help get the world back to normal.

I went to ask either Dafydd or Lily if there was anything *I* could do for the greater good, but Lily shooed me into the games room, promising to talk to me later. So instead, I decided to set up a game of chess, like Ettie had asked a while ago.

The lid to the box of chess pieces was jammed. It was a small, ancient-looking wooden box where the lid slid off in one direction but . . . I could see the problem. A piece of paper had been wedged inside and the lid rammed closed, catching on it. With a bit of force and thumb effort, I managed to free it.

What annoying person stuck—

My brain didn't finish the thought, because the folded piece of lined paper had my name written hastily on the outside.

I glanced about the room. Everyone was busy – reading, playing other games, chatting. Jos was singing 'jingle bells, Batman smells', and my new opponent, Ettie, was still at the dinner table. I opened up the note.

There was a room key taped to the paper and around it, in spidery writing:

My xmas gift to you: knowledge is power
theres a camera in the star on the Christmas tree
Told you theyre watching
T

22

WILD THINGS

28 December

I stared open-mouthed at the note for a beat too long, and suddenly I wasn't alone.

'Ready to play, Masen?' Ettie sat down and started setting up the black pieces.

Cold fear prickled along my spine.

They're watching.

Did that mean spying, or just like CCTV?

I shoved the note and the key into my pocket, quickly set up the white pieces and moved my pawn to D4, giving me time to think. An idea came to me.

'Did you hear barking just then?' I came up with a quick lie. 'I think it's Kika, my uncle's dog. I haven't walked her enough because of the rain.' I stood up. 'Play in half an hour?'

'Sure,' said Ettie, disappointed.

'Sorry. I've been neglecting her a bit lately,' I said and left, making sure no one saw me head up the stairs and not to the barn.

Did I look weird? Was I behaving strangely?

To anyone who might be watching.

Try not to think about that.

One. Step. At. A. Time.

Yes, that's what I needed to do. Mum wasn't here to remind me, so I had to do it myself. Step one: T stood for Tam, so this was their room key.

I took the stairs two at a time, then, with shaking hands, fumbled the key to the door, but eventually I was in . . . someone else's room! I felt like a criminal. A terrified criminal. What was I doing? Why was I here?

Why had Tam given me their room key? Tam said when they were anxious, they got curious. They wanted to know everything . . . but everything about what? The safe house not being safe? What did that even mean?

I sat on the bed, closed my eyes and counted to

ten. I imagined Mum and Dad behind me, a hand on each shoulder. Telling me everything was going to be OK.

Relax. Open your eyes. What do you see?

I let myself go floppy and observed the room, not looking *for* anything, just looking.

This wasn't 'Tam's room', especially now they'd left, so it wasn't any good searching for something of . . . *Oh.*

On the chest of drawers was that book Tam had mentioned: *Where the Wild Things Are*, the one where Max's mum calls him 'Wild Thing'. It was at an angle, not lying flat, and when I went to pick it up I saw it was hiding something: the radio from downstairs.

As I picked it up the back fell off, and a load of Post-it notes fell out. I grabbed them before they fell to the floor and shoved them in my back pocket. What was left was just the shell of a radio, with nothing inside it to make it work. However, *beside* it was a little pink music player, one of those old-fashioned 'pod' ones. I pressed the button and it began to play.

'This is a safety announcement from South Wales

Police. Until further notice, all members of the public should remain in their homes, keep warm, and avoid the roads until the danger has passed. Do not try to follow or divert any infected persons. They will be assisted by the emergency services. This is a safety announcement from South Wales Police . . .'

It ran on a loop. It sounded real enough, but the fact that Tam had left it for me to find made me suspicious. Was it a recording from the radio? It couldn't be – the radio was fake. And why did Tam have it? How? I was sure they thought this was a brilliant clue to whatever they were worried about, but I was more confused than ever.

This was all probably nothing – the result of Tam's overactive imagination – but I heard Mum's voice in my head telling me to trust my feelings. And they were telling me to be careful.

I decided not to mention the radio or the message to anyone, but I did want to dig a little deeper, and respect Tam's gift of information.

It took me ages to find Gloria – Lily said she'd disappeared for a while – but eventually, I tracked her down in the garden.

'What were you and Tam talking about so secretively this morning? Before they left,' I asked her, as we walked towards the barn with a treat for Kika.

She frowned at me. 'Nosy, much?'

I flushed. 'I'm not being nosy. I just . . . did they seem all right to you?'

Gloria was silent for a long time and I wondered if she'd heard me, or if she didn't want to. But then she shook her head and sighed.

'They seemed fine to me. And if you must know, Tam was showing me a photo of their parents. Happy?'

I'd upset her. Perhaps I hadn't been clear enough. 'It's just . . . is it possible Tam thought something strange was happening here?'

'People are infected with a fungus.' Gloria stepped away from me, creating a gap between us. 'Is that the sort of strange you mean?'

'No, I don't mean out there. I mean . . . in here,' I said. 'Something not quite right?'

She ducked under the large oak in the middle of the lawn and crossed her arms. 'In here? In my dad's house?' Her jaw clenched. 'My dad's trying to help. Look after everyone. What are you saying?'

I swallowed. This was not going as I'd intended.

What was I trying to say?

'Tam just seemed—'

'Tam was fine. Perhaps it's you who's got a problem? Stop looking for something to be wrong. You're overthinking everything.' She stormed off and I leant forward, hands on my knees. I was a terrible person. The world was falling to bits but there were still people who cared. People who would open their house to strangers and feed them and look after them. How had I got this so wrong? Gloria was right, I'd let my thoughts run wild. I took off my glasses and wiped my eyes. Then I stuffed my hands in my pockets to stop them shaking. In one pocket was Tam's key, and in the other, Mum's compass. Both made me feel calmer just touching them.

Mum used to say that I might not always understand people and they might not understand me, but I was good at noticing the little things. Perhaps I spent so long trying to figure out what people were trying to say without actually saying it, that I'd become an expert. Tam had taken a risk trusting me with what they'd found, so perhaps I needed to trust myself. Gloria and Tam were very different people but they did have one thing in common: they were both scared. *That* was what had been wrong with Tam when Avi, Keren and Yasmin left. They weren't just sad about it; they were terrified.

23

NOTED

28 December

I'd almost forgotten the Post-it notes until I sat down for dinner and felt the wodge of paper in my back pocket. I needed to look at them alone . . . I needed some time to *be* alone, so after a delicious plate of fish and chips, I made a genius suggestion that Jos have a sleepover that night with his new best friends in room 17, siblings Leena and Leo.

With Jos safely down the hall, I sat on my bed, alone, and dumped the Post-it notes on the duvet. Tam had numbered each of them, so I started reading in order.

1. 25/12 helped unload a bunch of food

Weird medical equipment also delivered
Dafydd shooed me away from it and called me nosy

Tam wrote like they spoke, without punctuation or pauses.

2. 26/12 Dr H told Keren theyd picked up her dad from their house on Christmas Day that cant be true coz she was Home Alone (thats not a joke btw)
she wasnt supposed to tell anyone her dad was at a party in Swansea & if the roads are all blocked how did he get home

(then in different colour pen)

3. 26/12 Found a mini security camera in the Christmas tree star
Going to search for others

(different colour pen again)

found cameras in library hidden behind old book:

The Day of the Triffids
in tinsel by chess set
in plain sight on top of tv!!!
4. 26/12 Dr H told me they had a lead to find my dad in a pop-up hospital
Havent seen my da in three years
Hes in spain

5. 27/12 OMG managed to get signal before phone died Got BBC news No mention of infection AT ALL Normal news like Best of the year lists (obvs written by someone with no taste)
Wales news: power outages – difficult to restore power because of Storm Elena
nothing about EVERY SINGLE ADULT PERSON BEING A MUSHROOM ZOMBIE

6. 27/12 asked a few people about mushroom-trees in their houses
All had them delivered as a gift from a 'secret santa' same as us
Who is this killer Father Christmas

7. 27/12 Tried to leave last night across old friary
dafydd found me in a flash
they are watching us all
I think theyre going to make me disappear
will leave a note for that new kid hes smart
is he smart enough to figure out what they want
with us tho

The final note made my head swim. It all read like a mad conspiracy theory, except for the fact that Tam *had* disappeared without any of the ceremony of Avi, Keren and Yasmin. No saying goodbye, no hot chocolate, just a story about their gran. Was Tam making connections where there were none? Was I? It *was* a speciality of mine. Sure, Mum said I had a knack for seeing what was going on beneath the surface, but then she also said I sometimes 'put two and two together and got Friday'.

Can I really trust my instincts?

If Keren's dad wasn't in hospital and Dr H lied about finding Tam's dad, then where were they now? Or was it all easily explained by a bigger picture and a bunch of tired grown-ups mixing people's relations up?

It was time to ask myself who and what I believed in. But I couldn't hold all my thoughts at once and they spilt across my brain like scattered seeds. I gripped my hair with my hands. This had to be our safe space, otherwise what did we have? Surely no one, *no one* would be cruel enough to use this disaster to . . . to what? And with kids?

It's nothing – just a strange sequence of events, made stranger by fear and uncertainty.

But if it were a sinister plot, wouldn't a national calamity be the perfect opportunity to take advantage of?

Then I remembered something and my blood froze. How could I not have realized? On Boxing Day, when everything had been so scary and confused, Gloria said all the roads were blocked – same story as everyone. Except Dr H said my parents were probably in A and E, and that the emergency services were on their way for the people on the cliff. Helicopters AND ambulances, he'd said. Can helicopters fly in storm-force winds? And how were these ambulances getting through? Maybe it was just another mistake. Or maybe he was lying. And if he was lying about that . . .

I let the thought hang there, wondering where it would end up, but I never found out. The lights went off and someone in the hallway screamed.

I grabbed the crumpled notes and stuffed them back in my jeans pocket. Then I stumbled in the near-dark towards the door. A thin wash of light from the window guided my way, but my heart was hammering and the gloom and shadows only made it worse. Then, my unhelpful brain started giving an Oscar-worthy performance:

They're on to you too, they can read your thoughts, any minute now you'll feel a bag go over your head and you'll be bundled into the back of a car and taken to the beach for the Infected to feast on. They have to eat, right? Dr H loves his mushroomy plants, and it needs to feed, they need to feed . . .

Shut up!

I exploded through the door and on to the crowded landing. The rest of the kids were all emerging calmly from their rooms.

My chest heaved as I tried to catch my breath.

Gloria ran to me with a torch in her hand, the light bouncing off walls and the ceiling. 'You OK, Mase? You look like you've seen a ghost.' She put the torch under her chin. 'WoooOOOooo!' She burst out laughing and it was too much. What on earth was going on?

'Seriously, Masen . . . are you all right?'

I stared back at her. I must've looked like a right muppet, but I had no control over my face, my body.

'The power's run out, is all. Dafydd's gone to see if he can find more genny fuel . . . for the generator.' She handed me a cup of hot chocolate from a tray beside her.

I nodded, the use of my muscles gradually returning. 'Yeah, genny, I get it.' I sipped the comforting chocolate and smiled at her, suddenly overwhelmed with sadness that I'd thought badly of these people who had done nothing more than save our lives. Whatever was going on, it couldn't be anything to do with them. Gloria was smiling like our conversation from earlier was forgotten. Like she'd forgiven me already, and I felt like such a terrible person. She was being a much better friend than I was, and if she'd got cross before, well she was just scared, like the rest of us.

A kid behind me groaned. 'That's the end of the

PlayStation then,' she said. 'And the DVDs.'

'And the pool,' grumbled another.

'Dafydd will sort us out,' said Gloria, chiding. 'And good to know you've got your priorities straight – don't worry about cooking or heating, hey?' She ruffled a kid's hair.

A low mumble came from the gathering.

'Go on then,' said Gloria. 'Back to your rooms. Might as well sleep – there's nothing else to do. Open your curtains if you need a night light – the moon is almost full. You can dream of bread and water for breakfast.' She laughed again and I felt even more silly for panicking.

Gloria bounced along the hallway and back downstairs, the light from her torch dancing across the tinsel. I thought back to our first meeting – she hadn't had to help us out in that muddy field, or rescue me and Conor from the dunes. A bad person just wouldn't do those things. I yawned, suddenly incredibly tired. Things would make more sense in the morning. They usually did.

24

SEARCHING FOR MORE THAN ANSWERS

29 December

The night passed easily, although my dreams were full of wild, dark landscapes and darker thoughts. I woke feeling groggy and ragged.

I got out of bed reluctantly. The room was cold and I desperately wanted to stay put. My eyes were heavy and I could've gone back to sleep, but I felt an urgent need to check on Jos. I couldn't understand why I hadn't looked for him last night after the power cut.

It was so unlike me, but I'd felt unbelievably sleepy.

The sleepover idea wasn't feeling so clever now and I wouldn't be able to settle until I'd seen him.

With all this on my mind, it was a while before I thought about Tam's notes. I only vaguely remembered getting into bed again last night, and my jeans weren't on the floor where I thought I'd chucked them. I checked the bathroom, but they weren't there either. Instead, a fresh pair of joggers and hoody lay folded on the chair by the window.

If my jeans were gone, then so were the notes . . .

But could someone really have come into my room in the night and taken them, honestly? I was a light sleeper at the best of times and with all the bad dreams I was having, surely I'd have woken up – the slightest noise or movement would have startled me.

I was furious with myself for being so tired as to not remember.

I breathed out heavily, creating a tiny cloud in the cold air, and remembered the power was out.

Bread and water for breakfast.

If only Dr H would find Mum and Dad. Gloria said they should've been in hospital early on, as our cottage was close to the coast, so what was taking so long? I needed to get out . . . it felt like I was losing my mind.

The mood at breakfast was different to usual. Instead of chirpy energy, a heavy quiet hung over everyone. The kids were sat around with duvets draped over shoulders and wearing hats and scarves. No one had much to say apart from 'pass the jam' and 'don't hog the blanket!' and 'are you going to finish those Hooplas?' It was less busy than usual too and I guessed some of the kids had chosen to stay in the warmth of their beds.

'Morning,' I said, as I sat at the table and poured myself some apple juice from a carton, forcing a smile.

'Good morning, Masen,' said Lily. She didn't need to force her smile – it was always there, glued to her permanently happy face. 'What a night, eh? I'm glad I managed to get *some* laundry done before we lost power. You lot were getting a bit pongy!' She nodded at me in my fresh outfit. So, she had taken my jeans? She showed no trace of having seen Tam's incriminating notes. 'And Dafydd went out first thing this morning to scour South Wales for something to put in the generator. He thinks we can get it to run on cooking oil if needs be, but hopefully it won't come to that.' She waved her hand in front of her face to indicate that would probably smell quite bad.

'I wish he'd hurry up!' snapped the hungry Hooplas fan.

Everyone gasped. To my knowledge, no one had ever barked at Lily like that. She was too nice. Lily's smile wavered but didn't fail. 'Enough of that, thank you, Andrew.'

Nerves were fraying.

Is that all it takes to wear us down? A few comforts gone: no hot food and dead batteries?

Andrew rocketed to standing, knocking over his bowl of dry cereal. 'You can't talk to me like that, you're not my mum!'

Andrew's roommate pulled at his sleeve. 'Andy, sit down and shut up.'

The kid opposite mimicked him. 'Yeah, Aaaandy, shut up.'

Andrew's lips wobbled against the rage, unable to form words, and, not content with spilling his breakfast, he swept an arm across the table, sending cups and bowls flying.

'I hate you. All of you. Go get mushroomed.' He sobbed. 'Just leave me alone.' He kicked back his chair and ran from the room, as Lily tried to right the crockery before too many precious resources were lost.

It was only then that, to my shame, I noticed Jos wasn't there.

'Leena? Where's Jos?' I kept my voice level with some effort.

Leena looked over at her brother. 'He got out of bed before us, I think. He did warn us he was an early riser, bless him.'

Leo just shrugged.

'Neither of you have seen him then?' It came out shrill. I didn't care. 'Lily, have you seen Jos?'

Lily was on her way out of the room, presumably to see to Andrew and calm him down. She was so good at that sort of thing.

'Sorry, Masen, I haven't. Just give me a few minutes.' She barely looked round as she hurried into the hall.

Leena looked anxiously at me, as if I was about to flip over my breakfast, too. 'I'm sure he's around, Masen. Try not to worry. It's been a weird morning. Maybe he's outside?'

I blinked back the urge to grab everyone in the

room and shake them and demand they think about my brother. Instead, I nodded calmly. 'He might be.' I tried to convince myself that he actually might be – he was a pretty outdoorsy kid, and the atmosphere was pretty weird in here, and . . . and . . .

Yeah, right.

I walked quickly, not running, calling for Jos in a forced-casual kind of way. He wasn't near the pool, or the gazebo, or the tree, or the split hedge. And he wasn't in the allotment . . . but Dafydd was.

'Hey, Dafydd! I thought you were out looking for fuel . . . or cooking oil?'

Dafydd blinked in confusion. 'No. I've been here all morning tending my beauties. They're the answer to all our problems, Masen. Look after the plants and they will look after you.' He frowned. 'Fuel for what?'

'The generator.' My heart squeezed in my chest. What was going on?

Dafydd stared at me for a beat too long. 'Ahh, the genny – yes, of course, that's all sorted. No need to worry about that. I "borrowed" a load of diesel from a tank in a farm over the hill. First thing this morning. All sorted.' He picked a fat slug from a baby cabbage and threw it over the hedge. 'Why, is the power not back on yet?'

I shook my head without saying anything, trying to communicate and think at the same time. *Is everybody lying to me or am I just paranoid?*

Dafydd chuckled. 'Bloomin' scientists! Dr H might be a genius but he can't even change a light-bulb. I'd better go and sort it out.'

Did I believe him? I wasn't sure. 'Have you seen my brother, Jos?'

Dafydd looked across the lawn to the horizon and beyond. 'Don't think so. I'll tell him you're looking for him if I do.' He ruffled my hair. 'Chin up, lad, everything's going to be fine.'

But it wasn't. And by lunchtime, Jos was still missing.

25

HIDDEN THINGS

29 December

Lily made me a cup of sweet tea that she said would calm me down and told me to wait in the kitchen. But I couldn't. I needed to walk, to pace away the panic, and I could use a hug from Kika, too.

I walked across the garden, clutching my hot tea to steady my hands, and heard voices in the barn as I approached.

I tiptoed the rest of the way to the door and crouched below the window next to it, which was ajar to let fresh air in for Kika.

I heard Gloria first. 'This has gone too far. I don't agree to this.'

'Yes you do. Or you wouldn't have brought them here.' That was Lily's voice.

'I had no choice,' hissed Gloria.

'What does your dad like to say? There's always a choice,' said Lily. 'The choice he's made wasn't an easy one, and we knew there would be sacrifices along the way, but he's doing something wonderful for the world. I know you understand that. When I met him, he was a broken man, devastated, just like I'd been. Now look at him. Look at me.'

Kika barked from inside the barn. I wondered if she could smell me.

'What about Dafydd?' Gloria sounded cross. 'Did he agree to this *choice*?'

'That's different,' said Lily. 'Dafydd made his own bed, now he has to lie in it. Come on, there's work to do. The weather's improving and we're running out of time.'

Footsteps moved towards the door and I edged around the back of the barn, making my escape behind the old friary ruins. My foot twisted on something metal protruding from the ground and I stumbled, twisting my ankle. I looked down and saw I'd tripped on a couple of bent tent pegs. I thought of Conor, getting his Glasto tent. I hoped he was OK.

I took the long way round past the allotment, which was empty, and back to the house.

And met Lily and Gloria outside the back door.

'Been for a walk?' said Lily, with an arched eyebrow.

'Just to the allotments. To ask Dafydd if he'd seen Jos.'

'Dafydd and Dr H have taken the BMW to search for your brother,' said Lily. 'Don't you fret. He'll turn up.'

Gloria squeezed my arm. 'Why don't you play with Kika, take your mind off things.' She pulled me in for a hug. 'Maybe Jos was playing hide and seek and found an amazing spot. I once hid for so long, I fell asleep.' Gloria's suggestion, though well-meaning, was little comfort, and her cheerfulness sounded fake. No one had said they were playing with Jos, not hide and seek or any other game, and he'd vanished early – before his sleepover friends had even woken.

No, this was not a game. This was something else.

I handed Gloria my tea mug. I badly wanted to ask her about her dad being a 'broken man', or about what she didn't agree with, but last time I'd asked questions, they'd upset her.

She said it was better not to think.

'Gloria, I'm sorry about before.'

'No. I'm the one who should be sorry. I shouldn't have snapped at you.'

My stomach unknotted a little.

She glanced around. 'I haven't been entirely honest.'

I held my breath.

'Tam *was* showing me a picture of their family, but that's not the whole story. I wanted to see them because I had a family too. A brother – James. He was a bit older than me and he . . . well, he died in an accident when he was seventeen. Dad has been trying to find a . . . a cure for what killed him ever since. He's getting really close and then all this happened and he's been busier than ever, so I was cranky . . .'

I gasped. 'I'm so sorry, Gloria. I'm sorry if I pushed you into telling me that.'

'It's OK. We're friends, right? I don't know why I

didn't want to mention it. I'm just a bit all over the place.'

I leant closer. She smelt of flowers. 'Of course. And we're definitely friends.' Poor Gloria. I couldn't imagine being without Jos. 'Is it OK to ask how your brother died? Is that too personal?'

Gloria fiddled with her hair. 'Not personal, just . . . complicated. Look, I have to go help Lily but I'm absolutely sure Jossy will be fine. He can't have got far. Do you trust me?'

I nodded.

'Good, now go be with Kika. She looked sad earlier.' She patted my arm and went into the kitchen.

As I watched her go, I thought about how much I actually did trust her. She was definitely hiding something: '*I don't agree to this*' played on my mind, but if they were talking about her brother then it made sense. That must be what her dad was 'devastated' about. I tried to imagine Gloria as part of some conspiracy and it just didn't fit. She was a fourteen-year-old kid dealing with a crisis, not some supervillain.

Still, just in case someone *was* watching, I went

into the barn, scratched Kika behind the ears, then doubled back. I was trying to figure out what to do next when the horrible smell of burning hit my nose. It seemed to be coming from the allotment.

I crept around the side of the house towards a thin line of smoke rising from behind the greenhouse, and I was about to investigate when something caught my eye behind the plexiglass.

Nestled between a stack of plastic pots and a roll of twine was a phone in a fluffy purple case, covered with shiny charms.

Dafydd's greenhouse was sickly warm and heavy with humid air and the aroma of things growing. It was a weird clash of sensations against the chill I felt in my blood as I picked up Tam's phone.

Why has Dafydd got this?

And what had Lily meant when she said 'Dafydd has made his bed'?

Assuming Dafydd was actually looking for Jos, he could return any moment.

I should've run, but instead, I went further in, through the greenhouse to Dafydd's shed. The smell of soil, tea and paint filled the air.

There was a cluttered desk on one side, piled high with non-fiction books about mushrooms. One had a bookmark stuck in the middle and I opened it to the marked page. There was a black and white drawing of trees and plants above ground and fungi below, with a huge underground network that linked everything together. The author had labelled it: *the internet of fungi*. The trees and flowers seemed to be using it too. It looked awesome, but also . . . a bit worrying. I wasn't sure I liked the idea of fungi being that clever, that in control of things on the surface.

I closed the book and made sure it was exactly how I'd found it.

Beside the books was a clutter of other items – paintbrushes and other art supplies (I remembered Dafydd saying he loved to paint), an ID card for Swansea University genetics lab, a photo of a young woman.

What was I doing? So what if he had Tam's phone? They'd probably dropped it. It didn't mean anything bad had happened to them . . . or that he'd have something of Jossy's.

But I kept looking anyway.

I felt like I was playing that game where you have to spot the odd or missing item. But everything seemed pretty normal for what I knew of Dafydd: secateurs, paint palettes . . . and a leatherbound journal.

I opened it carefully and found all the pages had been torn out apart from a half sheet, left behind in haste.

Meet: Fellow of Botanical Studies
East Wing 4FL
Monday 2 p.m.
Serenity trials

Then an arrow and

Tell Cara – she'll love this

Where were the rest of the pages?

The smell of burning!

It was literally what had drawn me here and I hadn't found where it was coming from. I ran outside, following my nose, and found an old rusty metal bin containing the remnants of smouldering papers. It looked like someone – probably Dafydd – had tried to burn the contents of his notebook, but the rain had put it out. Now it was dry again, it had begun to smoke.

I grabbed a poker leaning against the bin and pushed the papers around. Pages and pages of paintings and writing – dates and numbers, graphs and charts.

I grabbed what was left of them, shaking off bits of ash, but then movement caught my eye. I flicked my gaze to the polytunnel immediately on my left as a dark shape swiftly moved out of sight – someone had been watching.

26

DATA

29 December

There was a rustle from the shrubby border and then someone whispered, 'Mase?'

It was Gloria.

My heart stopped trying to kill me and I breathed out, long and slow, and she crept into view.

'Way to give me a heart attack,' I scolded. 'How did you know I was here? Is your dad back?'

'No. What have you got there?'

I couldn't hide the pages now, so I fanned them out on the path for her to see. 'It looks like Dafydd was trying to get rid of these,' I said.

Among the pages of data were small watercolour

paintings of plants. I recognized the style, they were just like *Serenity One* – the painting from the staircase on Boxing Day. They all had the same artist's squiggle in the corner: *DEJ*.

'These are his paintings,' said Gloria, sadly. 'Dafydd Elis Jones. But why would he burn them? They're beautiful.'

They were. The detail of the brightly coloured plants and fungi was extraordinary. Dafydd clearly loved his subjects, cared about them . . . he was always in the allotment with his 'beauties'. I brushed ash from three of the paintings, labelled *Serenity Two*, *Serenity Three* and *Serenity Final*: a tiny Christmas tree with bright, rubbery blooms. Underneath he'd pencilled in a scientific name: *Passiflora mycota nativitatis*.

The mushroom-tree!

I laid out the paintings in order and it was like they showed a timeline of the plants and the mushrooms growing together, becoming one thing.

A thought was forming. Was Dafydd responsible for making the trees? Was he the 'killer Father Christmas' from Tam's notes?

'Dafydd is mad about plants, and I found loads

of fungi books in his shed.' I had an idea. 'What if you can't choose between the things you love . . . like peanut butter and Marmite?' I was talking too fast, but I had to get it out. 'So you have both.'

Gloria looked baffled. 'You're not making any sense.'

'What if Dafydd crossed his favourite plants with his favourite mushrooms and made something awful? Like a peanut butter and Marmite sandwich.'

Gloria just stared, her leg jiggling anxiously.

'He's written something about "Serenity trials" in an old journal. Trials mean testing, right? Testing if you can combine plants and fungi. But why?'

And why would it infect people?

But it had. '*Serenity Final* is the mushroom-tree that infected everyone. It's right here!'

Gloria leant close to me. 'No! They must've found it. No one would make something so dangerous.' She looked annoyed with me, like I was accusing Dafydd of something awful, like I'd almost accused her dad. Which was exactly what I was doing.

But this time I know I'm right.

Something occurred to me. I stood and, without anywhere else to put them, stuffed the pages inside the pocket of my hoody. 'Come with me, but walk casually, like we're just chilling.'

Totally relaxed and not awkwardly at all, we went back into the house, to the main foyer. I'd remembered there were certificates of achievement on the walls among the portraits and photographs, all decorated with plants from the garden.

'What are you looking for?' whispered Gloria.

'Here!' I dragged Gloria to the wall beside the front door and pushed aside a tendril of ivy. 'Look, it reads: "Dafydd Elis Jones, University of Swansea, blah blah, advances in the field of mycogenetics and psychology". I think myco means fungi, so the first bit means genetics of mushrooms. What about the psychology part?'

'I think it's to do with how brains work, how we think, how we feel . . . how you can trick the brain and change how people think.'

I looked around, trying to push aside the thought that someone might be watching . . . or listening. 'Is it possible that Dafydd *made* the mushroom-tree and then did trials on it to make it affect people's brains?'

Don't think about the ant.

Gloria bit her lip. 'But why would Dafydd do that?' She paced back and forth. 'We need to get out of here,' she said. 'Don't suppose you know how to drive, do you?'

I shook my head. 'We can't leave. Tam tried it and Dafydd found them and dragged them back. They said we are all being watched.'

Gloria looked up to the top of the huge Christmas tree and at the corners of the room.

'We have to think of something.'

Keys rattled in the old front door, and beside me Gloria jumped out of her skin as Dafydd strolled in. I felt certain he could hear my heart hammering.

'Gloria?' He cocked his head at her, and I telepathically willed her to stop looking so utterly terrified. 'Are you OK? Oh . . .' He looked down at his muddy wellies on the clean tiled floor. 'Oops. Did you . . .?'

Gloria seemed to gather her wits and switched seamlessly to mock fury. 'Yes, I did, Dafydd Jones. Mopped it with my bare hands just this morning. What are you like?' She looked at me and laughed, still stiff, but relaxing into the role.

I remembered my own part: 'Did you find Jos?' I

asked, trying to look hopeful. I also looked concerned but I didn't have to fake that.

Dafydd slipped his boots off and pinched the tops together, holding them by what looked like the only clean patch. 'No, lad. I'm sorry. I'm going to head out over the fields to look for him there. Try not to worry.'

But Gloria had fallen back out of character. She was looking manically at me again, and I just stared back at her, wishing she would relax. She blinked several times.

I was pretty sure things were getting weird – although I wasn't the best judge – and then Lily called to Gloria from the kitchen, asking her to help out with Will, who was having a meltdown.

'You know he only calms down if you're there. Read him a book, will you?'

Gloria was still looking at me with wide eyes. It was like she'd short-circuited, and it was making me even more alarmed.

What is going on?

'Quickly then, Gloria,' pressed Lily, looking uncertain too, perhaps as confused by Gloria's expression as I was.

Gloria cringed at me, apology in her eyes, then followed Lily through the kitchen doors.

Why was I so good at spotting the little things and not the glaringly obvious?

'I think Gloria was trying to draw your attention to *those*.' Dafydd's expression went from calm to furious lightning fast. He pointed at the pages of his notebook poking out from my hoody.

The world dropped away from under me.

27

IN THE HOT HOUSE

29 December

Dafydd swiped the papers from their appallingly bad hiding place, then grabbed me by the arm. We strode urgently through the dining room and out of the back door, all the time my brain screaming at me to shout for help, but I was too scared . . . and too embarrassed – the room was full of kids, they'd think I was just upset like Andrew.

I stumbled along beside Dafydd, through the garden and on towards the old friary ruins.

This is it.

No one will know where I've gone, either.

With my free hand, I reached into my pocket

and grabbed Mum's compass for comfort. My most precious item.

I love you, Mum.

I dropped it by the hedge, hoping someone might come looking for me and find it.

We stopped by a knobbly, ancient stump of stone and Dafydd told me to sit.

'You like plants?' asked Dafydd, again.

This time I nodded, too terrified to reply.

'And you like art. I remember.'

I swallowed. It was bitingly cold but my whole body was alive with sweat. I wanted to wipe my forehead but I was rigid.

'I'm sorry – I . . .' I was no good at lying, so I gave up trying.

Dafydd put a hand on my shoulder. 'Did you read it, or just look at the paintings?'

Tears pooled. 'Just the paintings. The numbers and charts didn't mean anything to me. I'm sorry . . . please don't . . .'

Don't what?

What did I imagine he was going to do?

Dafydd ran his hand through his hair. 'I'm not going to hurt you, Masen, if that's what you're worried about. I'm not like them, not really.' He sighed. 'Will you let me explain?'

I was too scared to say no, so I nodded. 'Good.' He breathed out fog, then began, 'I like plants *and* art; you've probably worked that out by now. And fungi. I went to study at Swansea University and joined a group investigating how climate change was having a strange effect on some of the plants in Brazil – I painted some of my best pieces over there.' He sighed, perhaps at the thought of them ruined now.

I found a little courage and asked, 'What kind of strange effects?'

'Do you know what hybrids are?'

I thought of a peanut butter and Marmite sandwich and felt sick. 'I think so. Living things merging with each other to create new species. So you *found* the mushroom Christmas trees? You didn't make them? 'Cause I know that's what infected everyone.'

Careful, Mase.

There I went again, asking too-blunt questions. But tiny fir trees in the rainforest didn't seem right to me.

Dafydd looked like he was thinking very

carefully about what to say next. 'Sort of. We found hybrid fungi-plants . . . they seemed to affect everything around them. We brought them back to the lab for—'

'Genetic engineering?' I mumbled, ignoring my own advice to take care.

'Testing.'

I picked a lump of lichen off the knobbly stone. 'Why are you telling me this?' I didn't look at him; I couldn't. The phrase 'I could tell you, but then I'd have to kill you' popped into my head. People always say that as a joke, but it didn't sound funny *at all*.

'Because this has gone too far.' He put his face in his hands and his shoulders shuddered like he was crying. 'You shouldn't be here. None of us should, and I've had enough. I've already said too much. I only wanted to warn you that they're on to you. It's why they took Jos—'

'Where is he?' This time I did look at him, wildfire in my eyes. 'If you've hurt him I'll—'

'He's OK. They won't hurt him, that's not their plan. Believe it or not, they don't want to hurt anyone, especially kids, but . . . they won't let you get in their way either, and you ask too many questions.' He sighed. 'I don't want to be part of it any more. People have got hurt and it's getting out of hand.'

'Who?' I demanded. 'Who is "they"? How did Serenity get into people's houses?'

Dafydd looked shocked as he shushed me. 'Listen, I can help you, but you've got to stop poking your nose into things. Meet me at the allotment at five o'clock tomorrow morning. Wrap up warm. I'll get you out of here, then you run; find the police.'

'Why can't we go now? Wait . . . I thought there weren't any police? Aren't all the adults . . . *infected*?'

Dafydd's eyes darted about nervously. 'This isn't what you think. Look, I've said too much already. Now, do you want my help or not?'

I stared in silence.

He stood and put his hands on his hips. 'Right, off you pop then, I imagine it'll be ice cream time soon.'

I blinked several times, stuck to the spot, then calmly turned like nothing had happened, and walked back towards the house that was supposed to be my sanctuary.

*

They're on to you. It was on repeat in my brain. I didn't know where to look, what to say, what to do. I lost four games of chess in a row with Ettie and she got bored and went to do cartwheels in the garden.

I itched with wanting to talk to Gloria but she'd vanished again, so I pretended to read a book, all the time listening to conversations that floated my way – people waiting to leave, excitement that the power had been restored, dismay that it was rationed to one hour a day which meant no electronic devices whatsoever. No hope of charging phones, no browsing photos of loved ones, no music or gaming.

And no way of knowing if anyone can get a signal. Why is that?

Just enough time to cook a hot meal, but there were complaints about that too. Too many vegetables. Not enough sweets. Except for the fake Fabs; they kept coming.

Gloria found me mid-afternoon. She seemed relieved to see me and dragged me into the middle of the lawn to talk, so the mysterious *they* couldn't lip-read. I told her in close whispers about Dafydd's plan for the morning, then I pushed my luck with the question I *had* to ask. 'Gloria, are you absolutely sure your dad and Lily don't know anything about this? About Serenity.' I couldn't help but think of whatever I'd half overheard in the barn.

She grabbed my hand. 'My dad's a doctor – he took what's called the Hippocratic Oath. It means he's not allowed to hurt people. And Lily . . . she's just too sweet. So are her lads.' Gloria leant back on her hands and breathed out heavily. 'Whoever it was, they can't have meant for this to happen.'

We stared at our feet.

'Can I come with you tomorrow morning?' Gloria whispered into my ear.

I took her hand. 'Yes. PLEASE.'

If we could just make it to dawn, we'd be free. What we would do after that I wasn't sure. We'd need a new plan. I'd have to put my faith in what was left of humanity and trust that not everyone was infected, as Tam had hinted at in their notes. I had to hope that the people who had done this could be stopped. I also had to trust Dafydd, when he said they wouldn't hurt my little Jossy.

28

THINGS CHANGE

30 December

I didn't sleep. My watch and phone were dead so I couldn't set an alarm. Instead, I sat and watched the clock by the bed until four thirty. Then I put on an extra layer – two T-shirts from Lily's laundry pile and a hoody – and crept down the stairs, shoes in hand, hoping upon hope that no one else was creeping around the house in the dark.

I eased open the back door; the only sound was the faint rustle of tinsel in the cold air. Once outside, I slipped on my trainers and, under a cloud-heavy sky, moved quietly through the dewy silence to the allotments, where I ducked down and waited. There was no sound. No birds, no traffic noise, no sign of any life at all. The world felt dead.

By comparison, my breathing was as loud as an orchestra and Gloria's footfalls were thunder!

'Mase?' she whispered.

'Here,' I replied. 'Brussels sprouts.' I eased myself out from behind the veggies.

'No Dafydd yet?'

I shook my head as she peered through the dark at her old analogue watch. 'We're early, though.'

Early, late, it made no odds – Dafydd didn't come for us, and by six we were stiff, cold and forced to accept that we were not making our escape that day.

We returned to the house with no choice but to act like all was normal. I ate a little at breakfast and huddled under a blanket, wondering if I'd ever be properly warm again. My bones felt cold. The other kids avoided catching my eye, but I knew they were all wondering about Jos. He was still missing and obviously not reunited with family, and something about that made them all feel unsafe. Everyone was on edge. Even Gloria fidgeted like she didn't know what to do with herself and I wondered if she was having second thoughts about her dad's involvement.

After lunch, Gloria and I returned to the greenhouse, putting on a front of bravery. Dafydd was there, spraying rows of newly planted seedlings with a fine mist. He didn't look up.

'What happened?' I demanded.

Dafydd didn't reply. 'Nothing's happened, just minding my plants.'

'That's not what I meant. You know what I meant,' I snapped.

Dafydd looked at Gloria.

'It's fine, you can trust her. She was going to come with me . . . *this morning*.'

Dafydd put down the spray but continued staring at the plants. He looked tired, confused, defeated.

'So? Where were you? We waited.'

Next to the seedlings was the photo of the woman, the one I'd seen in the shed. He touched it gently, then he lifted his gaze to me.

'I'm not sure what you mean, Masen. I've got a lot to do here, so maybe run along back to the main house. You'll be fine, Lily's sons are out finding your parents. It'll be fine . . . soon enough . . .'

Of course.

They'd got to him too. Watching, listening. 'You're a coward,' I said. With one angry motion, I swept the pots of seedlings to the ground, spilling out soil and roots and hope along with them.

I ran back into the Friary and thundered up the stairs, ignoring Lily's calls to slow down and walk, ignoring the silence from the rest of the house, trying to fend off the scream rising in my chest. I burst into my room, threw myself on the bed and finally let it out into the pillow.

I don't know how long I wailed and raged and sobbed, but eventually, I was all cried out. I was so tired, so drained, so . . . done. I'd failed to escape, failed to protect Jos. There was nothing left to do. Nothing left but to wait for them to come and take me.

Eventually, a voice in my head drowned out the despair, and I was surprised to find it was Tam. I remembered our conversation about needing knowledge to feel safe, or powerful, and it sent a shiver of optimism through me. Better to die trying something than sit here and wait for my fate. It was such a bold thought that I almost didn't recognize myself as I sat up, ready to make a new plan. One where I found my brother.

Dafydd said they took him . . . what if all the kids who were 'reunited with their parents' were taken to the same place?

Dafydd also said they didn't want to hurt the kids, and I did believe him, because why keep us all here, feed us, entertain us, only to kill us days later?

'So, Tam, what knowledge do we have?' I felt silly talking to them out loud but it helped; the house was so quiet now. 'Does it matter if Dafydd made the mushroom-trees, or if they found them in South America?' It wasn't that I cared about solving the mystery of Serenity any more, but following the clues might lead me to Jos.

I imagined Tam saying, '*No – more important is why they wanted to turn everyone into mushroom-zombies.*'

'Especially as Dafydd said there's a cure. If this is a plan for world domination, it's pretty rubbish.'

I paced the room – there still wasn't much in the way of knowledge to go on. Nothing that led to Jos.

'There has to be a reason for making Serenity and then unleashing it on the world.' Or was it just

South Wales? I didn't even know that.

I wish you were here for real, Tam. I hope you're OK.

I went to reach for my compass and my heart sank as I realized it wasn't there. Instead, Mum's advice popped into my head: one step at a time.

OK, I can do this.

'They make Serenity, then get lucky with the cold.' I stop pacing. 'The Serenities die and everyone gets infected with fungus. Then they bring any kids left behind to the Friary and then . . . disappear them.'

There was one place I knew about round here where people disappeared – that gap in the hedge. Maybe that's what the palm-entry bunker was for. They *had* to be keeping the kids in there!

Including Jos. It felt like such a huge break-through that I jumped in the air and pumped my fists high—

The shriek of an alarm sliced through the house and I slammed my hands over my ears. An alarm like that meant only one thing.

Fire!

What was the drill? Leave immediately and gather on the lawn? Don't stop to collect anything.

Don't stop to worry if your missing little brother can get out of wherever he is, don't stop to let your imagination run away with thoughts of him trapped by flames.

But was this for real? The timing was seriously suspicious. But my brain made me follow the rules. And in a fire, you got out as quickly as possible.

I burst out of my room and ran down the corridor, sadly forgetting the most important rule of all, Mum's rule: one step at a time.

I tripped in the gloom of the unlit staircase and went down hard, twisting my ankle. My cheek slammed into one of the picture frames, leaving skin and blood behind and sending my glasses clattering to the floor. I pulled myself up on the banister, wincing in pain, blood stinging my eye and blurring my vision. Where was everyone? No one else was running, no one was in the hall. Just Lily on the stairs, to help me up.

'Lily . . .?'

I felt the sharp sting of a needle press into my skin. A push of fluid, invading my muscle until it was tense, and then . . .

Then . . .

29

TIME TO WAKE UP

30 December

'He's waking up.'

I don't want to. I'm warm and so sleepy.

'Damn it! His eyes are opening.'

No, they're not. They are stickyish and tired and I'm sleeeeepy.

'I told you the sedative wouldn't last long enough.'

Who is that?

There was light pressure on my chest, rubbing, rhythmic, and my eyes unglued. I opened one, letting in a little light, a little sight, and I realized that I hadn't been speaking aloud but in my head.

'What's going on? Where's Jos?' My voice was

thick with saliva. My head was thick too, like I'd slept heavily.

'He's coming back.'

Who? Me? Where had I been?

The sensations of my body returned one at a time. Dry mouth, banging head, painful arm . . . can't move the arm, more painful ankle. Then . . . memories. The fire, falling on the stairs, Lily, a needle—

I tried to sit up but only my torso moved – my arms were restrained, shackled to a narrow metal bed. Hands went to my shoulders. Strong hands, pushing me back down. My eyes defogged and I saw them, Dafydd and Lily.

No, no, no!

I was right . . . Tam was right. I struggled to move but they held me firm.

'Let me go!' I yelled, my voice cracking.

'Shh, there now. It's all going to be fine,' said Lily.

I'd suspected it, but now it was confirmed I couldn't accept it – Dafydd, Lily, they were so kind. What was happening to me? Was I injured? Or was I about to be? I tried to kick out but my ankles were bound too. The movement sent a spike of hot pain up my leg, which almost sent me into unconsciousness again.

I blinked, furiously. 'What are you doing? Let me go!'

Dafydd's warm Welsh voice poured into me like poisonous hot chocolate. 'I can't do that, Mase. I'm sorry.'

'Where's Jos? What have you done to him?'

And Keren, Yasmin and Avi. And Tam.

'Where is everyone else?'

'They're all fine. They're sleeping.' Dafydd cast his eyes over to my right where, through a curtain of hospital plastic, I could make out the shapes of beds in the room beyond, and people hooked up to IV bags. 'All just . . . helping out.' My sense returned enough to see that Dafydd was struggling with something. What was it? Guilt? A lie?

'What about Gloria?'

Dafydd nodded. 'Yes, she's here too, but . . .' He looked away, then he and Lily put on masks, and Lily wheeled in what looked like a hospital trolley.

'But what? What have you done to her?'

On the trolley was a large plastic box, and for a second I wondered if it contained test equipment –

things to read your blood pressure, oxygen, heart rate, that sort of thing. But no – they were being monitored behind me. I could hear the beeping and pinging and there were wires leading away from my body. Lily lifted the top off the box to reveal a plant. A huge, lush, leafy plant, at least as tall as me, and dotted all over with buds. I recognized them from the mushroom Christmas tree – Mum had said the petals were like Play-Doh. This was Serenity . . . upgraded.

30

JUST GIVE IN TO IT

30 December

I could've laughed at my ridiculous brain – the first thing I thought was how good Dafydd was with his plants, his 'beauties'.

And then, I screamed.

'Shh, Masen, honestly, it'll be fine,' said Lily. Unlike Dafydd, there was no sign of guilt or doubt on her face. She looked at me so caringly, like this would be good for me. Then I remembered what Gloria had said before . . . the 'greater good'. How could anyone possibly think *this* was good? I tried not to think about what had happened when Gareth got infected at the pub.

'What are you going to do?'

Then, Dr Haradwaith pushed through the curtain. 'We're going to take away all your troubles. It's really nothing to worry about. The "flowers" will bloom and you'll breathe in the spores, and then you'll be like the others, helping us perfect Serenity, making sure it works on everyone, even children. You're part of something wonderful, Masen. I promise you, when this experiment is done and we're heroes, you'll be pleased we let you take part.'

What?

Heroes? This was full-on villain behaviour.

'Dafydd, please help me.' I pleaded with my eyes. 'This isn't right, you know it.'

Dafydd looked like he was ready to be sick.

Dr Haradwaith's friendly face slipped. 'Stay where you are, Dafydd,' snapped the once-jolly Dr H. He turned to me. 'He won't help you because he does what he's told . . . or else. Why don't you tell the young lad here, Dafydd? Tell him what you did.'

Dafydd looked greener than his plants. 'I almost killed someone. My lab assistant. My friend.' His voice broke. 'She nearly died because . . .' He couldn't go on.

'Because your work during testing was sloppy.' Dr Haradwaith was almost snarling now. 'She was the first person ever infected by Serenity and it was a bit more . . . powerful back then. That poor girl – Cara – her poor family. Although . . . it did give me the idea for all this.'

Full-on SUPERvillain behaviour.

That explained why Dafydd was wrapped up in all this. So, Cara was the woman in his photo and Dr Haradwaith was blackmailing him. And this was no accident; they knew how dangerous Serenity was. And they carried on anyway, carried on *because* of it.

Anger was making me brave. 'Just so I understand, this is all for the greater good – whatever *that* means – and I'm going to be happy to be a zombie shambling to the sea? You're ridiculous.'

Dr Haradwaith laughed. He *actually* laughed. 'No, no, no. That was a mistake. We couldn't have predicted the storm, the power cut and the big freeze. Remarkable that just a small drop in temperature would kill them, even indoors.' He sat beside the bed, back to being the kindly doctor. 'None of that was meant to happen. You see, the spores aren't meant to take over your brain like the ant in the video. That was an extreme reaction to the cold. Serenity is a tropical hybrid and when it felt itself dying, it tried to save itself – a defence mechanism. Fascinating really, and tremendously useful data. Under normal conditions, Serenity is designed to slowly give out spores that alter your personality, help you remain calm. See, it's a good thing.' He sighed. 'There is so much stress and worry in the world today, Masen, especially in your generation. You scroll endlessly on your phones looking at apps literally designed to make you angry and afraid. You spiral into anxiety. And it's not just kids; everyone is divided, arguing, so stressed and distracted.' He slammed his fist on the trolley and Serenity shuddered. 'I want to stop that, which is why we MUST get Serenity to work on kids.' He touched the bruise on my head, gently, and my stomach rolled. 'You're part of my vision for the future, where everyone has Serenity in their homes, at the dinner table, beside the TV, in school. A calming influence in a hectic world.'

He spoke like he was filming an advert for his 'vision'.

‘It’ll be like any other product you can buy to reduce stress – like a meditation app, or a nice-smelling candle.’

I struggled in vain against the restraints. ‘That’s completely different. You can’t drug people. Aren’t you a doctor? You took that oath thing that means you can only help people.’

His expression changed again. ‘I am helping people. The world will be a better place for everyone.’

‘Even the people on the cliff?’ I spat.

Dr Haradwaith turned on his heels and stalked back to the curtain. ‘That wasn’t our fault.’ He flapped through the plastic and I felt a small rush at the tiny victory of getting under his skin.

Dafydd looked sick with regret. ‘I’m sorry, Mase. We didn’t know the consequences of Serenity suddenly dying. Unfortunately, it did exactly what the ant fungus does. It took over the infected people’s brains and “programmed” them to head south and get warm. I love my plants, I’d never killed one before. But don’t worry, I’ve made you a good one here. Good and safe.’ Head down, he pushed through the plastic curtain and out of the room.

Lily placed a hand on my forehead, perhaps to offer comfort, but it just made my skin crawl. 'It'll bloom soon. Then you'll sleep, like the others, and when you wake again, you'll see how calm you are, how peaceful. No more stress. No more anxiety.' Her eyes were full of peace. The most calm, serene person I'd ever met . . .

'You're infected, aren't you?' I said, with sudden realization.

Lily smiled, then she left too.

I craned my neck to look at the sleeping guinea pigs in the next room. My view was obscured by the cloudy plastic, but I could make out shape and colour. There were at least ten kids, maybe more – beyond the beds were more dark masses but they could have been almost anything. A huge Serenity plant was positioned in the centre of the room. The colours were unmistakable, big and bright . . . in other words: in bloom. Pumping out its pacifying spores. None of the kids were moving. They looked asleep, sedated or . . .

No. Not dead.

I swallowed down the thought and tugged uselessly at the wrist restraints. It sort of went without saying that I absolutely had to get out of there, but I couldn't do that tied to the bed. I didn't need toxic spores to control my anxiety, I could manage that like I always had: one step at a time. And the first step: figure a way out of the straps – something other than just pulling and tugging. I looked at what I might be able to reach. I stretched my fingers but only touched the bare black foam of the bed. Not very helpful. I stretched my neck, turned my head, even stuck out my tongue, but I couldn't reach anything.

And then it was too late.

More voices came from beyond the curtain, away from my stuffy little plastic room. Dr Haradwaith was back and he was shouting. And I could hear very well who he was shouting at.

Gloria.

31

HOW COULD YOU?

30 December

No.

It wasn't that I wanted Gloria to be a victim of Serenity – I didn't want her to be zombified by fungi. But I didn't want her to be involved, either.

Their voices grew louder as they approached.

'. . . outsiders. I told you not to bring them here.' That was Dr Haradwaith's voice. He was talking about me and Jos. 'We chose the people for the study very carefully. Local people. Goodness knows why Serenity ended up in an Airbnb – that was sloppy. And these two put everything at risk. And so have you.'

'But Dad—'

'No!' Dr Haradwaith clearly didn't care if I heard – in a few minutes I wouldn't care about much. 'Time is running out. The storm has passed, the power is back, internet, phones . . . the roads are being cleared as we speak. I can't keep blocking them with abandoned cars. The rest of Wales will be at our door any day now. Dafydd is cleaning up, burning all the remaining failed Christmas tree hybrids and getting rid of the evidence in the house.' There was a pause, then, 'Here's your passport. Go pack a bag. We'll continue the project from the South American lab . . . just in case.'

So the rest of the country, the world, isn't infected. I remembered Tam's Post-it saying the news had been normal on 27 December. *They were right again.*

'How is that all you can think about? Clearing up a mess? What about the people on the cliff? How will you explain that?'

'I won't need to – we won't be here, and *none* of this links back to us. Everyone infected on Christmas Eve will be recovering from the fungus by now. Their immune systems will have killed it off without a trace, and they won't remember a thing. Neither willl the kids. No one outside the project knows anything about Serenity. Apart from THAT BOY!' His voice was hot with fury. So much for preaching calm.

He pushed through into 'my' room and checked the plant. 'Won't be long now.'

I growled with the effort of struggling – I knew it was pointless but I didn't want them to think I'd given up. 'Gloria?'

She turned away from me.

Coward.

'You can't think you'll get away with this?' I snapped at them.

'Of course we will,' said Dr Haradwaith. 'You're the last loose end to tie up. When the others come round, they'll be told the same story we'll tell everyone. A mystery virus tore through our poor little community, but we're all fine now. Any mention of fungus zombies will be written off as fake news or conspiracy.' He met my eyes. 'Because without any evidence, who would believe it?'

Evidence?

'What about CCTV?' I said. 'There'll be footage of the people, the herd, the beach.'

Dr Haradwaith shook his head. 'No power,

remember. We've been so lucky.'

Gloria's expression slackened in shock. 'How can you call this lucky, Dad? People died. You never said that would happen.' She glanced at me like she wanted me to know that. Well, if she was trying to make me feel sorry for her, she had another thing coming. 'You said people would breathe in harmless spores and then fill out a questionnaire to say how calm they felt.'

'Don't be so naive, Gloria. This is cutting-edge science. Groundbreaking endeavours come with risk. Why do you think the first astronauts were animals? This is a dangerous business we're in, but don't forget it's all for—'

'The greater good. I know,' said Gloria, scowling.

'We're saving lives in the long run, and what could be more important than that?' said Dr Haradwaith.

'You really believe that, don't you?' What I couldn't believe was how he had told so many lies to us all.

Gloria stepped closer and checked my wrist restraints. Cold metal pressed against my skin and I almost snapped at her, but I didn't want to give her the satisfaction of seeing me upset.

'It won't bring back James,' she said to her dad. Dr Haradwaith glared at her and dragged her out through the curtain.

Alone again, I felt sicker than ever, and I didn't think it was the sedative. Gloria had lied about so much. SO much. Unforgivable lies about my family, about Jos, and the kids. And worse, I had confided in her. I told her everything, every step of the way. Conor said I was too trusting and it made me ache.

Her betrayal hurt, but worse was the shame. It spread over me like an infection, black and rotten – the shame of believing we were friends.

How could you?

Then, the Serenity beside me shimmied like it was waking up from a lovely nap, stretching, yawning, looking forward to a nice day's infecting people. The flowers were still half in bud, opening slowly, so I had some time . . . but how much?

I tugged at the restraints again but only succeeded in hurting my already bruised wrists.

I started to cry.

I missed my mum, my dad, my uncles, Nanny Sasha.

I missed Jos most of all. I was supposed to protect him and I'd let him down.

I miss my best friends, I miss Kika and Fran . . . I even miss Conor.

I wondered what it would be like to be infected and if it would hurt and if I'd still be me.

I thought about the Christmas presents still under the tree, and that when the buds opened up I wouldn't care about any of it any more.

No.

It was a switch flicking on.

One. Step. At. A. Time.

I wondered how far I could slide down the bed, perhaps reach something with my feet, but I was distracted by a sharp poke in the wrist, right where Gloria had touched me. I wished she hadn't done that – I didn't want to feel her or think of her . . .

I turned my left hand over to reveal a bent tent peg jammed against the metal bar of the bed.

The cold sensation I felt.

Could I use it to flick up the pin on the buckle? My hands were shaking, but I took a stab at it. Too fast. The tent peg shifted and I stopped mid-inhale.

Slowly does it.

Serenity flexed again, and a low-hanging flower creaked and cracked half open like popcorn in a pan. I held my breath and tried again. I got the pin free, pulled my arm back a little and then hooked the strap loose. It was still through the buckle and the tab, but now not pinned in place. It might be enough. Yanking my hand had done nothing but if I was careful and twisted slowly, slowly, slowly . . . the strap eased open a little; it was working!

Then, the pin flicked back and locked into place.

No!

Breathe.

Think.

The strap had loosened. Maybe it was enough. I tucked my thumb into my palm, made my hand as small as I could, and pulled.

The restraints had a woolly lining but that didn't make it any more comfortable. If anything, it was the opposite: it burnt my skin, friction fighting me as I twisted my hand, drawing it towards me slowly, but with enough force to squeeze through the slender space.

Another bud split open, the petals already glowing deep blue and pulsing. A hum built from deep within the bud, vibrating in time with the flash of purple and yellow tiger stripes.

As bright as the eyes of the Infected.

I focused on my hand.

Slowly and surely, Mase.

Then there was another popping sound and the biggest of the three blooms opened fully, violently, its stamen shuddering in place, rubbing together, increasing the hum. The air looked dusty and I felt sleepy all of a sudden. Maybe I could just rest for a bit. Escaping would be much easier after a nice sleep.

No!

I pulled my wrist as hard as I possibly could. My hand popped free and the pain jolted me from the effects of the spores. I hoped I could hang on long enough to get out of the bed.

As my eyelids grew heavy, I tried to focus on the facts, thinking of Tam again. Of the missing details. Only this time I wasn't fighting off anxiety, but Serenity.

Why not just straight out of the car and down to the lab? Why all the Fabs and the swimming and the piles of pastries? Why you, Gloria? Why did you lie to us all?

I imagined her looking hurt and it was quite satisfying. I imagined her full of fear, pity, self-loathing... Or was that what *I* felt because I'd failed Jos? I hadn't listened to Conor, I'd missed all the signs about Gloria . . . I was the one who'd brought us to this house of hell.

32

TOUGH CHOICES

30 December

With my left hand free it should've been easy to unbuckle the other wrist strap, but my hand was numb and floppy and my whole body felt heavy. I was also attached to a drip and the machines that monitored my vital signs. The monitor was easy to deal with – it was just a plastic peg on my index finger which I snatched off and threw aside . . . the drip was a different matter.

But there was no time to be squeamish. Serenity was already puffing its poison over me, and the machines were probably attached to an alarm somewhere. If they were, then I didn't have time to lie there feeling faint at the idea of removing a needle from the back of my hand.

It was a no-brainer. Squinting, so I only had to watch through half-closed eyes, I slid the needle out of my skin and left it dangling from the drip bag. Blood beaded on my hand as I freed myself from the remaining restraints, all the while trying to hold my breath for as long as possible. I didn't know if that would help but perhaps it was better than nothing.

My lungs were now burning as well as my wrists.

Putting all my weight on my good leg, I launched off the bed, sending the gurney slamming backwards into the medical trolley. The machine, now showing my heart rate as a flat line, clattered to the floor. The trolley with Serenity on it wobbled in place and I stared at the plant – *my plant* – with my mouth clamped shut.

No one came running.

Behind the bed was a pile of medical masks and I grabbed one and held it over my face without bothering to loop the straps around my ears. I snatched my glasses from beside the bed, took a big step away from the trolley and breathed.

Three deep, panicky breaths and I was OK; I

was still me. I looked again at the plant, which was head height to me now, still humming, popping, clicking.

This version of Serenity was certainly different – not a Christmas tree this time . . . this was the Happy New Year version. We stared each other down for a second before I looked for something sharp to kill it with, to cut off its big, show-offy head. A box of disposable scalpels lay on the equipment trolley and I grabbed one. I was just about to open the packet when my brain woke up and basically slapped me round the face.

Don't kill it!

Dying was what had set off the Christmas tree Serenity! As much as I wanted the thing dead, we were going to have to call it evens, live and let live.

I pocketed the scalpel and hobbled out of my guinea pig's prison.

My first instinct was to be selfish: get the hell out of there. I wouldn't be able to help anyone if I was caught and I wouldn't get a second chance. Like Dr Haradwaith said, I was a 'loose end'.

He won't let me leave here alive.

I was sure of it. And Gloria would probably get

her own zombie-making plant for helping me escape.

Did I care?

Of course I did. Maybe she hadn't known what her dad was doing, not completely. He was supposed to be her trusted adult, so she'd believed him. Did I forgive her, though? That was another question – one I was glad I didn't have the head-space for.

But I could feel the others pulling me back, whispering to me from their slumbers: Masen Williams . . . are you really going to leave us here like this? Are you really going to leave Jos?

Of course not.

I secured my mask and dashed to the first of the beds. This was a *person* lying there, not a vague shape, maybe alive, maybe dead. This was no maybe – this was Tam. And they were alive.

I checked them all: Keren, Yasmin, Avi – and six others, all breathing. Hearts beating a steady rhythm of bleeps that chimed out of turn and out of tune with the hum and crackle of the Serenity plants beside them. They had pads on their temples, attached to wires, and I guessed that somewhere, someone was recording their brain waves to see how calm they were. This was where all the generator power was going, then. No wonder there wasn't enough for fresh milk.

Jossy wasn't there. The shapes beyond the far bed were luggage – suitcases, and I remembered seeing one in Dafydd's wheelbarrow. How had I been so blind? All the kids' things that they'd packed up to bring with them, meet their families with. Then I realized – Dr Haradwaith and his gang had picked up all the other kids from their homes. They already knew their addresses, because that's where they'd delivered the Christmas trees.

The lies upon lies weighed me down and I wondered how even Dr Haradwaith, with his *greater good* reasoning, could believe his own deceptions. The cruelty was beyond my comprehension. For someone who wanted peace, he'd sure dished out a lot of violence.

I battled with myself over my next move. The kids were alive and in that sense at least, safe, so should I find Jos and risk being caught, or assume he was in another room like this, and try and escape to get help? Help seemed more likely now I knew the outside world was still functioning.

I ached for my little brother; the very thought of him, his name, his smile, his dependence on me almost overwhelmed me, but I couldn't let that happen. I thought about a time in the future when all this was over and he was safe but he knew I'd left him and resented me for it.

But I had to make peace with it. Because I'd rather he was alive and hated me than the alternative.

I buried the thought deep and returned to Mum's mantra. What was the next step? Look around. Something my subconscious had realized ages ago suddenly shouted at my conscious brain: there were no windows.

Of course! We're in the bunker.

I stumbled on my emotions as I realized Gloria hadn't 'found' the bunker door with me at all. And the Oscar for best supporting actress goes to . . . Gloria Haradwaith.

Liar.

I pushed my thoughts of her aside.

Need to find a door, and stairs. And hope this bunker isn't some enormous underground warren.

And I needed to do it all before anyone returned and found me missing.

33

LILY

30 December

I squeezed Tam's foot. 'You were right, and so brave,' I said to them. 'I'll be back, I promise,' I whispered to them all. 'I'm trying to think three steps ahead, Avi.' Their still bodies made me shiver. But not as much as the creaking, shimmering Serenity.

I pushed back through the plastic curtains and into the main room. There was a single door out which I assumed would be locked, but I tried the handle anyway – I could hardly believe it when the door swung open.

How can they be so confident in themselves? That no one will find them, no one will believe what they've done?

On the other side of the door, to the left, a narrow corridor led further into the complex. On my right were the stairs I'd been hoping to find. I dashed up them and recognized the bunker doors at the top.

And of course, *they* were locked. I knew that from being on the outside.

Me and Gloria were joking about there being cheese down here, and all the while this *was under our feet.*

On the wall was a familiar panel – face or finger-print scan, most likely. So that was that, then. No way out.

The urge to give up was strong. But no! There had to be a way. There had to be more steps to take. My inner compass pointed behind me and I went back down the stairs and along the corridor.

At the end was a door, which I eased open just enough to creep through. It led to an office, with a desk and a laptop connected to lots of screens. The screens displayed multiple boxes of wiggly lines – I guessed the brain waves of the Serenity-controlled kids – and one showed all the CCTV in the Friary, including some Tam hadn't found: outside the bunker and, of course, the greenhouse. Beside the laptop, a Santa mug full of coffee steamed on a coaster.

The rest of the room was piled with boxes of supplies: medical gloves, needles, bandages and—

A thud from somewhere in the bunker made my heart do a double beat, and I crept behind the boxes and ducked down.

Footsteps tapped past the door and I breathed a brief sigh of relief . . . but then they paused, shuffled and returned.

The door swung fully open.

'You may as well come out, Masen,' said Lily, calm and pleasant as ever. 'I can see you.'

I looked up at the boxes all around me. There was no way . . . she was bluffing.

'Please don't make me come and get you. Do I need to call Dr Haradwaith? Or Dafydd? They'll just be cross. Come out and come with me and it'll be fine.'

As quietly as I could, I slid the scalpel from my pocket, unpeeled the wrapping and held it tightly in my shaking fist. I had no idea what I would do with it, but holding it felt like a positive step.

Lily's shoes clacked closer to my hiding space. She wasn't bluffing.

How?

She turned and peered over the boxes to look right at me . . . no, she was looking at her phone. Then, she smiled and turned the screen to me.

'See. I know where you are.' Her phone showed a plan of the bunker, and me on it: a blue flashing dot. She zoomed out to show me about thirty other blue dots, not flashing, motionless in the outline of several other rooms. One of those blue dots was Jos.

I frowned. 'You're tracking us?'

She nodded, still smiling. 'No one can resist ice cream day.'

Curiosity overtook fear. 'I don't understand.'

'It's a simple chemical tracer in the Fabs. In the sprinkles. Gives off a harmless radiation signature. That's why we make sure you eat them nice and regularly. And they're delicious. But mostly so we can know where you all are. Keep you safe.'

Safe!

Tam was right – they were watching. In so many different ways.

Lily clicked her tongue. She'd seen the scalpel in

my hand.

'Now, what are you going to do with that, Masen?'

I stood, slowly, my ankle throbbing, and pointed the blade at her.

'I just want you to let me out,' I said.

Lily looked confused. 'But why? When we want to give you *such* a gift.' She pocketed her phone and held her hands out to me. 'I've seen how you struggle. Don't you want to be at peace?'

I thought of the other blue dots.

'I want to be *me*. Not a mindless fungus zombie.'

'No offence taken,' said Lily, and I remembered she was one of them. There was no point arguing with her.

Is that what Dr Haradwaith wants? No more emotions, no more individuality? For us all to just do as we're told?

The same old question bubbled up in me again and I couldn't help myself. 'Why?'

She blinked and I caught the briefest flash of emotion in her face. 'I lost a daughter. Dr Haradwaith lost his son,' she said. 'All because of other people's negative emotions – anger, frustration, stress, rage . . . well, road rage.' She said it all without expressing any feeling at all. 'I couldn't bear to see my boys so devastated by the loss of their sister; I had to do something . . . for all of us.'

Of course – her sons are under the influence of Serenity too.

'This way . . . is less painful.'

That caught me off guard and I felt bad for her. 'I'm really sorry, Lily. I can't imagine how horrible that must've been.' I understood, maybe better than a lot of people, what it was like to feel emotions that you wished could be switched off. I'd been so scared, so worried, every second since Christmas morning . . . I'd love to make those feelings go away. But not like this. 'This is wrong. I don't want to be like you. I want to feel things . . . all the things – happy and excited, but sad and scared too. You can't have one without the other.' I dropped the scalpel. 'Please? I just want to go home.'

Lily didn't budge, but her expression changed a tiny bit. Maybe the real Lily was still in there somewhere.

How can I reach her? How can I reason with a zombie?

I held my hands out to her to show that I wouldn't hurt her. 'Lily—'

I got no further. A loud clunk and a thud carried along the corridor – the sound of the bunker door opening.

Lily smiled.

34

HEADING IN THE RIGHT DIRECTION

30 December

Footsteps sounded on the stairs. More than one person, I thought. Dr Haradwaith. Dafydd.

Game over, Mase.

Lily held out her hand for me to take.

Not yet. Take another step.

With both hands, I pushed against the boxes. They weren't heavy but they were cumbersome enough to knock Lily backwards. It distracted her long enough for me to jump over the remaining stacks and run into the corridor.

I darted back towards the main room and stopped in my tracks at what I saw.

Or rather, who.

Gloria rushed at me like a wave on the beach and grabbed me by my bruised wrist. I yelled out in pain.

'Shh!' a voice hissed from above. 'Jeez, Masen, shut up! We're trying to do a stealth manoeuvre here.'

It took a moment for my brain to make the right connections, to figure out what I was seeing and hearing. The bunker door was open; someone was there, silhouetted in the bright daylight. Then I saw jorts, a pair of very muddy, high-end trainers, and stripy wellie socks, and it all clicked into place.

'Conor?'

He urged us to hurry and Gloria pulled me up the stairs, into the light and on to the path. Then Conor pulled me in for a massive bro-hug. 'It's good to see you, cuz,' he said. Like he meant it.

Never in a million years did I think I'd be so happy to see my cousin.

'We need to go.' Gloria slammed the bunker door closed and rolled a thick log on top.

'Jos!' I cried.

Conor put a finger to his lips. 'Help is on the way. Gloria says he's safe . . . more or less. I need to get you safe, too.' He put a hand on my shoulder.

'Thank you – I should've said it before and I'm sorry about that.'

I was gobsmacked.

'You came back for me . . . twice. First in the dunes, then in the pub. I wasn't very . . . grateful. But thanks.'

'You're welcome,' I said, then stumbled, too overwhelmed to take in what was happening.

Conor caught me. 'Listen, everyone's OK. The whole family. They're back at the cottage, waiting for us. Come on.'

Everyone's OK?

I almost couldn't believe it, but I felt the weight begin to lift.

Then, Conor beckoned me to follow him and Gloria.

I scowled. 'Not with her – she's one of them.' I didn't have to try to look hateful.

'We don't have time for this, Mase,' warned Conor. 'I know what she is. I know what she's done. But she's helping us, so get a move on.'

I didn't see that I had much of a choice – it was either go with them or stick around to get zombified. There was just one problem.

'Guys, we can't hide from them – they can track me.'

'I know,' said Conor. 'That's fine. We have no intention of hiding. Although . . .' He looked at his watch. 'We might have to stall them a bit – I wasn't expecting to find you so soon. Or so lively. You got yourself free?' He clapped me on the back as though he were proud of me.

'Gloria helped,' I said, begrudgingly.

'Not much.' She gave Conor a hesitant smile. 'Just thought one of your many bent tent pegs might come in handy.'

Conor rolled his eyes. 'Guess I need more practice putting my tent up before Glastonbury.'

'Glastonbury?' *I tripped over tent pegs by the ruins, after I overheard Gloria and Lily talking in the barn. Had Conor been camping out here?* 'So it's true? The fungus zombies are just in Wales?'

Conor put his arm around me to help me walk as we crossed the grass. 'Not even that. Just here. Just the Gower. Just where we *had* to come on holiday. The evil doctor's experiment might have been dastardly, but it was small.'

'Five hundred households, Dad said. Not

many . . . some of them were our friends—' Gloria burst into tears.

On hearing that the world was OK, and the family safe, my energy left me. Suddenly, everything seemed to hurt, and I was more tired than I'd ever been in my whole life. With Conor's help, I limped behind Gloria, past the raised beds of leeks and onions and the greenhouse. I thought of Dafydd, head down, spraying his seedlings. I got that he'd been put in a difficult position and been blackmailed, but those were the exact times you got to decide who you were and what you stood for. Dafydd had picked the wrong side.

We stumbled out on to the gravel drive.

And came face to face with Dr Haradwaith.

Gloria scraped to a halt in front of her dad.

'Now, where do you think you're going?' said the doctor.

Does he mean me, or Gloria?

'Away from here,' Gloria answered for us all, through her tears. 'James wouldn't have wanted this, Dad. Neither do I.'

Dr Haradwaith adjusted his expression from angry to the warm, kind man I'd met at the campsite.

'Gloria, my love, I know you think that. I know you think we should move on, put our grief aside, but this is our chance to make a difference. Changing the world was never going to be easy. Scientific advances don't happen in a straight line. We have to try and try again. This time, I think we've got it right. Why don't you and your friends come inside, out of the cold.'

I couldn't believe what I was hearing.

Neither could Conor, apparently. He crossed his arms and faced the doctor. 'Are you deranged? You're not advancing anything. Gloria told me about James . . . your son. He sounds way smarter than you.'

I looked at Conor in disbelief. Why was he taunting Dr Death? Was he trying to make him angry? Then Conor gave me this hidden flicker of a wink and I remembered he'd said something about stalling.

He's waiting for something.

Dr Haradwaith's expression flicked back to rage. 'What do you know about anything?' he spat. 'You're just kids. How dare you challenge me? My brilliant son . . .' His voice, like ice, cracked. 'Yes, he was smart. Who knows what he could've achieved? But his life was cut short because someone ran him off the road. Driving angry, late for work, stressed, frustrated, then . . . a moment of madness. I don't blame the driver, I blame society. Serenity will fix it.'

'But you've killed people too,' I shouted. 'People just like your son.' I didn't know what Conor's plan was but I needed Dr Haradwaith to hear me. 'You're the one who's angry.'

Dr Haradwaith had the decency to look pained. 'It got out of hand. But this version will be better. Look, what's done is done. There's no need to waste all the data. The people on the cliff, their sacrifice will be—'

He never got the chance to finish whatever nonsense was on his mind, as a car screeched on to the drive, spraying gravel in all directions.

The passenger-side door swung open and Alys stepped out, baseball bat swinging in one hand, phone recording video in the other. For a moment, I wondered who was driving, then Big Lad Gareth opened the other door and emerged. I'd forgotten how intimidating he was.

'There's my little lad,' he said, giving me a wink.

My legs wobbled, but then barking came from the back of the car and there was a flurry of legs and tails as two burly dogs fought their way over the front seats and out of the doors.

Kika! Fran!

The pair charged me, easily pushing me over. I didn't care. The only thing that mattered was the flurry of licks and woofs. Alys turned to me, Gloria and Conor. 'You three – in the car.' Then she looked sternly at the dogs. 'And you. I told youse to stay in the back.' She pointed at the open doors. 'Go!'

Fran and Kika did as they were told, and so did we. Then, even though he'd only had a handful of driving lessons, Conor climbed in the driver's seat, seeming more mature and confident than I'd ever seen him.

Dr Haradwaith was on his phone, backing away from the new arrivals, his eyes darting about for an exit. 'Dafydd? Get to the front drive, NOW! Dafydd? Dafydd? Damn him.' Dr Haradwaith shoved the phone away and yelled towards the car. 'Gloria! What have you done?' He looked from the car, to Gareth, to Alys, who was still swinging the bat, and for the first time, he looked nervous.

Alys and Gareth strolled casually towards Dr Haradwaith.

'Dr Fungus, is it?' said Gareth. In the back of the car, I let out a terrified snigger. 'I'd stay back if I was a smart little doctor. Otherwise, Alys here is likely to get a bit . . . smashy.' He pushed up his sleeves and cracked his knuckles. 'She's not very happy about what you did to me.' Dr Haradwaith's mouth fell open and he turned and ran.

'He won't get far,' said Conor, and in the distance I heard sirens. 'Told you everything would be OK,' he said.

Gloria and I huddled in the back of the car, a Labrador each to keep us warm. She hadn't said a word since we got in – not when all the ambulances and police cars began rolling in, not when we heard that Lily's sons had been arrested on the beach, not even when Conor said that her mum was on her way to take her home.

'They'll want to speak to you,' Conor said to me. 'If you can manage.' I sniffed. I just wanted to go home. 'You've been really brave, cuz,' he said, holding out a fist. I bumped it. We'd never fist-bumped before.

'Not brave enough to rescue Jos.' I buried my face in Fran's fur.

'We've got that covered, mate. Don't worry.'

From the back seat, we watched Alys and Gareth talk to the police, saw two officers put Dafydd in the back of a police car; then the paramedics brought all the kids out. The second I spotted Jos, I leapt out and ran to him. He looked so small on the trolley and – I shivered to think it – peaceful. I squeezed his hand and he smiled, still fast asleep.

'He'll be fine,' said the paramedic wheeling him into the ambulance. 'They're all sleeping off the effects. We've accessed the Friary's medical data, so we've already given them the anti-fungal medicine. You'll see him soon.' I remembered that Dr Haradwaith had said the fungus would leave no trace once it was gone. At least that was something.

Another paramedic checked me over, and then Gloria and I had to answer a ton of questions with different police officers. I was numb. After all the emotions I'd been through, I didn't have any left. All the steps were taken. Eventually, we were allowed to leave and Conor drove us away from the Friary.

Gloria kept her gaze fixed out of the window. 'I'm sorry, Mase. I know that's not close to being enough, but I am. Really, really sorry. Dad wasn't who I thought.'

I wasn't in the mood for an apology. What I wanted was an explanation before we dropped Gloria at the local police station.

'How could you look me in the eyes and look so scared and worried and confused? When all along, you knew what your dad was doing.' Mum said I was a good judge of character and I had to know if she was wrong about me.

'Oh Masen, I *was* scared and worried and confused. I still am.'

'Don't be too hard on her, Mase,' said Conor. 'It took all of us to crack this thing. We might not have got to you all in time without Gloria's help.' He threw something over his shoulder to me and I caught it, smiling for the first time in what felt like ages. 'Gloria found it by the ruins and gave it to me. I knew you'd be lost without it.'

Mum's compass.

I flicked it open. It didn't matter which way was north, I was heading in the right direction.

35

HAPPY NEW YEAR!

1 January

At 5 p.m., the outside light came on automatically, and I practically jumped out of my skin. I was so focused on watching for the car out of the window that I didn't see them walking up the path. They must've driven round the back.

'They're here!' I yelled and Mum leapt up from the sofa and dashed to the kitchen.

'Kettle's on,' she called, after a moment of running water and clattering. 'Jossy, can you get the door, love.'

With a flourish, Jos swept the front door of our North London house open and, with a sense of importance, invited everyone in.

I hovered in the back of our hallway, unsure where to put myself, not that it mattered – I was tugged into a cuddle by Suzie the moment she clapped eyes on me.

'Come on, Masen – give yer bestie aunty a hug. It's good to see you!'

I melted into her embrace, all perfume and coffee and night air.

'You're more handsome than ever!' She turned to Mum. 'Isn't he just so beautiful, Tay?'

Despite the tiredness lines under her eyes, Mum glowed and brushed her hand across my cheek. 'He's perfect.'

I felt the comfort of her words through her fingers. People had called me 'heroic' and 'brave', but Mum said I was – and always had been – just perfect as I was.

Conor helped Nanny Sasha over the step, supporting her elbow as she entered to a round of applause from us all. Conor fist-bumped me with his free hand . . . Nanny Sasha did the same.

'This way, Nanny,' said Jos, puffed up and proud. 'You can sit here, in the chair of honour.'

Nanny Sasha winked at him and let him help her

into the seat. From her look, I could tell she was perfectly capable of doing it by herself, but she could see what it meant to Jos to be able to help. He'd grown up so much in the past week. Too much. It broke my heart to think of it, so mostly I tried not to. If he was angry with me for leaving him behind, he didn't show it; I wished with all my might that it would stay like that, but who knew what the long-term consequences of our horror Christmas would be?

Mum came into the front room with a tray of biscuits and tea and coffee, and we dived in.

'Mase gets the first biscuit, right?' said Uncle Bradlee. 'Our hero of the hour.'

Nanny Sasha caught my eye; she understood how I felt about all the attention.

'Nonsense,' she said. 'I'm the one with the broken bones. Need to keep my strength up.' She leant over, grabbed my least favourite biscuit: the shortbread, and winked at me.

I'd thought leaving the Friary would be the end to my ordeal, but I'd been wrong. I just wanted everything to go back to normal as soon as possible, but I didn't get much of a say in it – the news was everywhere and it was like my family had to go over it all again. Interviews, questions, photographs, statements . . . but I was grateful for it too because it meant we were OK. They'd all suffered minor hypothermia from being outside – they were rescued from the beach, but apart from that no one could remember anything of their journey – and Nanny Sasha had a broken wrist. All in all, they were better than most. Plenty of people had been more badly injured or lost. Thank goodness it had been confined to the Gower, and only the households to which Dr Haradwaith had delivered the trees.

Even away from the news, I saw *him* all the time. My dreams were full of dark underground corridors with locked doors, and giant ants with needles coming out of their heads. And he was always there, holding a mug of the hot chocolate they'd used to drug us each night to stop us going walkabout.

Conor waved his hand in front of my face. 'Oi! Pass us a custard cream, yer waste of space.'

I mate-punched him on the arm and passed the plate. 'Get it yourself, slacker.'

'Don't you eat all my recovery biscuits, you boys,'

Nanny Sasha scolded. She hopped up out of her chair, as nimble as you like, and grabbed the plate. 'Your dad told me you're a bit of a hero too, our Conor.'

Conor beamed and I happily passed him the baton of attention. We'd found a lot of common ground since that awful Christmas morning, but one thing that definitely set us apart was how much Conor enjoyed the limelight. He rubbed his hands together in glee.

'Well, Nanny, while brave Sir Masen here was uncovering the entire Serenity conspiracy, I was in my trusty Glasto tent, with my friend Alys, staking the place out, trying to figure how to rescue everyone.'

Aunty Suzie squeezed herself on the sofa next to him. 'Budge up, Con. Make room for your mum. Now, carry on, I never get tired of hearing about my super sleuth.' She stroked his hair, revealing a now-yellow bruise on his forehead.

'Super?' I scoffed. 'Is that why I saw you skulking around the hedge in the middle of the night?'

'At least I wasn't stumbling around like . . . what did we call them, Mase? The worst zombies ever?'

Aunty Suzie snorted and elbowed him. She dealt with her experience by joking around, but I saw the haunted look in her eyes. The fungus was gone, but we were all fighting to be ourselves again, to stop being under the influence of the devastating experiments of Dr Owain Haradwaith, because it had been so easy, too easy, to bring us all down.

'It was lucky I met Alys and Gareth . . .'

Conor and I exchanged a glance. I hadn't mentioned the pub and I never would.

He continued, 'Poor bloke, we had to lock him in his camper van to keep him safe, but eventually we got past the roadblocks on Alys's bike and sussed right away something weird was happening.'

Aunty Suzie butted in again. 'Alys is studying journalism and has a nose for a good story. It's her photos all over the internet, you know? Unbelievable!'

Conor raised his eyebrows at her. 'I was just getting to that.'

This was my favourite part of the story. While Conor and Alys were spying on the Friary, taking pictures of Dafydd, Lily and her sons and working with Gloria to download the data as evidence, I was inside, and at my lowest ebb. I'd known we were in trouble and I felt so alone. I know hindsight doesn't really count, but still, home and safe, it felt good to know that someone had been out there, literally looking out for us.

My phone buzzed.

Happy New Year! I hope your nanny's OK

Gloria. The last two days had been a rush, getting our things, getting home – 'as far away from that place as possible,' Mum said – but I'd decided to try and forgive Gloria, so before she went home to her mum's I'd got her phone number. Mum and Dad weren't happy about it but as Conor said, without Gloria's help, it might have gone differently. They'd teamed up the day Jos 'disappeared' – Gloria thought her dad had gone too far with that. Apparently, she'd spotted Conor's stripy socks a few days earlier (super sleuth indeed!) and from there, they'd hatched the plan to bring the project crashing down, together. I thought back to Lily telling me that she couldn't find Gloria . . . because Gloria was with Conor. So, despite some almost unforgivable lies, she wasn't *really* the villain. A bit like Dafydd, Lily and her kids, caught up in something bigger than all of them. Her dad, on the other hand . . . sometimes I tried to see his side of things and consider what I would do if someone hurt Jos, but the answer was never 'turn people into zombies' so he's absolutely a monster, in my opinion.

Besides, with her dad charged with murder and kidnapping, Gloria wasn't exactly in a good place, and she needed all the friends she could get. I remembered that feeling of isolation from the Friary.

The doorbell rang and finally the last of our guests arrived. Barking announced the presence of Kika and Fran, and the uncles.

Dad ushered them all into the lounge and handed Aunty Suzie a bottle of champagne, which she popped without even letting the new arrivals take off their jackets.

We all shouted, 'Happy New Year!' as Suzie poured fizz for the grown-ups and Pepsi for me and Jos. Jos took a too-big swig and burped loudly. Nanny Sasha burped too and we laughed like we hadn't laughed since before Christmas, all of a week ago.

'Got the PlayStation you asked for, then?' said

Conor, nodding towards the TV. I switched it on and saw that Tam and Avi were online. I'd try and get a game in with them later.

'Want to play?' I asked Conor, handing him a controller.

He scrolled through the downloaded games. 'Ha! Shall we play *ZombieFried*?'

I stared at him. 'Please tell me you're kidding.'

ACKNOWLEDGEMENTS

Christmas.

A time for peace, joy, goodwill to all . . . even zombies.

Some story ideas creep up on you. This one has been festering since I was about twelve, when my dad handed me a copy of *The Day of the Triffids*. (I still have it – 1981 edition, complete with a dreadful TV tie-in cover.)

I was hooked, particularly on the concept of waking up to silence, and ever since, I've dreamt of writing a children's book inspired by Triffids. Now, thanks to everyone at Chicken House, that dream has shambled to life. I hope you enjoy it.

The cover, in this case, is ridiculously brilliant – thank you, Tom Clohosy Cole, for capturing the sinister spirit of the season so perfectly.

The inside wouldn't be what it is without my incredible editor, Shalu (thank you for embracing my fungus zombies . . . though not literally!), the whole Chicken House team and Fraser Crichton.

Big thanks also to my brilliant agents, Callen and Lauren; Swaggers and Rebels; my writing rocks, Stuart and Emma; and, always, my family.

And to booksellers, librarians and teachers – thank you in advance for helping this spooky little story find its way into the world.

Finally, to you, dear reader:

Merry Christmas – and a spooky New Year.

TRY ANOTHER GREAT BOOK FROM EMMA READ

THE HOUSETRAP

Amity has run off into Badwell Woods. Her brother Claude goes after her, only to discover his little sister's scarf dangling near a house in the trees. Has she gone inside? He enters, not expecting a three-storey building with NO stairs. And a party laid out when there's nobody else around. Only when the front door locks behind him does he realize it's a housetrap. And they've been caught . . .

Gloriously spooky and utterly splendid.
HANA TOOKE

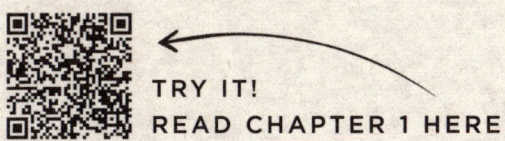

TRY IT!
READ CHAPTER 1 HERE

Paperback, ISBN 978-1-913322-78-6, £7.99 • ebook, ISBN 978-1-915026-71-2, £7.99

TRY ANOTHER GREAT BOOK FROM CHICKEN HOUSE

THE ZOMBIE PROJECT by ALICE NUTTALL

In a world without bees, death-flies are needed to grow food. But death-flies need bodies – lots of them. And bodies mean zombies.

Merian understands this, but others are afraid. Can one girl prove that zombies are the future?

Really sparky . . . an original talent.
CRESSIDA COWELL

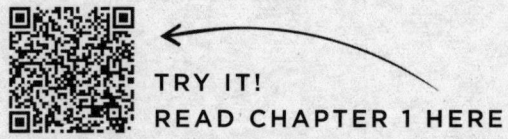

TRY IT!
READ CHAPTER 1 HERE

Paperback, ISBN 978-1-915947-34-5, £7.99 • ebook, ISBN 978-1-915947-35-2, £7.99

TRY ANOTHER GREAT BOOK FROM CHICKEN HOUSE

THE SCREAM OF THE WHISTLE by
EMILY RANDALL-JONES

Ruby is miserable. Her parents have split up, and now she's stuck in a creepy village. At night, she decides to escape and follow the ancient train track home.

Her journey has barely begun when she hears the eerie scream of a whistle – and an old steam train appears out of the darkness . . .

Is Ruby ready for the ghost ride of her life?

A spookily thrilling adventure laced with the perfect amount of fear.
JASBINDER BILAN

TRY IT!
READ CHAPTER 1 HERE

Paperback, ISBN 978-1-915947-14-7, £7.99 • ebook, ISBN 978-1-917171-17-5, £7.99